CRITICAL ACCLAIM FOR ROBERT B. PARKER

'Parker writes old-time, stripped-to-the-bone, hard-boiled school of Chandler… His novels are funny, smart and highly entertaining… There's no writer I'd rather take on an aeroplane'
– *Sunday Telegraph*

'Parker packs more meaning into a whispered 'yeah' than most writers can pack into a page'
– *Sunday Times*

'Why Robert Parker's not better known in Britain is a mystery. His best series featuring Boston-based PI Spenser is a triumph of style and substance'
– *Daily Mirror*

'Robert B. Parker is one of the greats of the American hard-boiled genre'
– *Guardian*

'Nobody does it better than Parker…'
– *Sunday Times*

'Parker's sentences flow with as much wit, grace and assurance as ever, and Stone is a complex and consistently interesting new protagonist'
– *Newsday*

'If Robert B. Parker doesn't blow it, in the new series he set up in *Night Passage* and continues with *Trouble in Paradise*, he could go places and take the kind of risks that wouldn't be seemly in his popular Spenser stories'
– **Marilyn Stasio**, *New York Times*

THE SPENSER NOVELS

The Godwulf Manuscript
God Save the Child
Mortal Stakes
Promised Land
The Judas Goat
Looking for Rachel Wallace
Early Autumn
A Savage Place
Ceremony
The Widening Gyre
Valediction
A Catskill Eagle
Taming a Sea-Horse
Pale Kings and Princes
Crimson Joy
Playmates
Stardust
Pastime
Double Deuce
Paper Doll
Walking Shadow
Thin Air

Chance
Small Vices*
Sudden Mischief*
Hush Money*
Hugger Mugger*
Potshot*
Widow's Walk*
Back Story*
Bad Business*
Cold Service*
School Days*
Dream Girl
   (aka Hundred-Dollar Baby)*
Now & Then*
Rough Weather
The Professional
Painted Ladies
Sixkill
Lullaby (by Ace Atkins)
Wonderland (by Ace Atkins)*
Silent Night (by Helen Brann)*

THE JESSE STONE MYSTERIES

Night Passage*
Trouble in Paradise*
Death in Paradise*
Stone Cold*
Sea Change*
High Profile*
Stranger in Paradise

Night and Day
Split Image
Fool Me Twice (by Michael Brandman)
Killing the Blues (by Michael
   Brandman)
**Damned If You Do (by Michael
   Brandman)***

THE SUNNY RANDALL MYSTERIES

Family Honor*
Perish Twice*
Shrink Rap*

Melancholy Baby*
Blue Screen*
Spare Change*

ALSO BY ROBERT B PARKER

Training with Weights
(with John R. Marsh)
Three Weeks in Spring
(with Joan Parker)
Wilderness
Love and Glory
Poodle Springs
(and Raymond Chandler)
Perchance to Dream

A Year at the Races (with Joan Parker)
All Our Yesterdays
Gunman's Rhapsody
Double Play*
Appaloosa
Resolution
Brimstone
Blue Eyed Devil
Ironhorse (by Robert Knott)

***Available from No Exit Press**

ROBERT B. PARKER

DEATH IN PARADISE

A JESSE STONE MYSTERY

NO EXIT PRESS

This edition published in 2014 by No Exit Press
Harpenden, Herts, UK

First published in the UK in 2002
by No Exit Press,
an imprint of Oldcastle Books

noexit.co.uk
@NoExitPress

A CIP catalogue record for this book is available from the British Library.

ISBN
978-1-84344-221-9 (print)
978-1-84344-222-6 (epub)

16 18 20 19 17

Typeset in 11.5pt Minion by Avocet Typeset, Somerton, Somerset
Printed and bound by 4edge, Hockley, Essex

FOR DAVE AND DAN

who kept their mother going
and brought their father home.

1

One out. A left-handed hitter with an inside-out swing. The ball would slice away from him toward third. Jesse took a step to his right. The next pitch was inside and chest high and the batter yanked it down the first baseline, over the bag and into the right-field corner, had there been a corner, and lumbered into second base without a throw.

'I saw you move into the hole,' the batter said to Jesse.

'Foiled again, Paulie.'

They played three nights a week under the lights on the west side of town beside a lake, wearing team tee shirts and hats. One umpire. No stealing. No spikes allowed. Officially it was the Paradise Men's Softball League, but Jesse often thought of it as the Boys of Evening. The next batter was right-handed and Jesse knew he pulled everything. He stayed in the hole. On a two-one count the right-handed hitter rammed the ball a step to Jesse's left. One step. Left foot first, right foot turned, glove on the ground. Soft hands. Don't grab at it. Let it come to you. It was all muscle memory. Exact movements, rehearsed since childhood, and deeply visceral, somatically choreographed by the movement of the ball. With the ball hit in front of him, Paulie tried to go to third. In a continuous sequence of motion, Jesse swiped him with his glove as he went by, then threw the runner out at first.

'Never try to advance on a ball hit in front of you,' Paulie said as they walked off the field.

'I've heard that,' Jesse said.

His shoulder hurt, as it always did when he threw. And he knew, as he always knew, that the throw was not a big-league throw. Before he got hurt, the ball used to hum when he threw it, used to make a little snarly hiss as it went across the infield.

After the game they drank beer in the parking lot. Jesse was careful with the beer. Hanging around in the late twilight after a ball game drinking club soda just didn't work. But booze was too easy for Jesse. It went down too gently, made him feel too integrated. Jesse felt that it wasn't seemly for the police chief to get publicly hammered. So he had learned in the last few years to approach it very carefully.

The talk was of double plays, and games played long ago, and plays at the plate, and sex. Talk of sex and baseball was the best of all possible talk. Jesse sipped a little of the beer. Beer from an ice-filled cooler was the best way for beer to be. From the edge of the lake a voice said, 'Jesse, get over here.'

The voice was scared. Carrying a can of Lite beer, Jesse walked to the lakeside. Two men were squatting on their heels at the edge of the water. In front of them, floating facedown, was something that used to be a girl.

2

The rest of the Paradise cops didn't like looking at the body. Jesse had pulled it out, and it lay now on the ground illuminated by the headlights of the Paradise Police cruisers.

'She been in the water a long time?' Suitcase Simpson asked Jesse.

'Yeah,' Jesse said. 'She's only wearing one shoe.'

Simpson didn't look. He didn't care about how many shoes she had.

'You seen a lot of floaters?'

'When I worked in L.A., there was a lot of oceanfront,' Jesse said. He was squatting on his heels beside the corpse, studying it. He reached over and turned the head a little and studied it some more.

Simpson was trying to look at the body obliquely, so it would only be an impression. He was a big kid, with red cheeks and some baby fat still left. But he wanted to be a cop. He wanted to be like Jesse. And he was trying to force himself to look, the way Jesse did, at the water-ridden thing on the ground.

Behind them, Peter Perkins had strung crime-scene tape, and behind it the Boys of Evening stood silently, looking at the scene, but not the body. There was no talk. As they stood, the town ambulance pulled into the parking lot with its lights flashing, but no siren.

Through his open window the driver shouted to Jesse.

'Whaddya need?'

'Body bag.'

'You're sure?'

'Yes.'

The two EMTs got out of the ambulance without shutting off the flashing lights. They got the litter from the back and lay a body bag on it and wheeled it over. Neither of them liked looking at the corpse.

'Drowned?'

'I don't think so,' Jesse said.

He moved her sodden hair and pointed with a pencil. 'Bullet went in here, I think,' Jesse said.

'A bullet?'

'Yep, went out the other side. No need to look. Let's roll her in the bag.'

Still trying to look without seeing, Simpson said, 'You thinking she was murdered, Jesse?'

'I'm thinking she was shot in the head behind her right ear and the bullet exited high on the left side of her head and blew a pretty sizable piece of her skull off when it did.'

'Maybe she shot herself,' Simpson said.

'And jumped into the lake after,' Jesse said.

'So you're saying she was murdered and her body dumped?'

'It's a working theory,' Jesse said.

3

Jesse sat in his office with his feet on the desk and talked with the State Police Homicide boss, a captain named Healy.

'The homicide commander personally?' Jesse said.

Healy smiled.

'I told you,' he said, 'I live in the neighborhood.'

'You got the pathology report?'

Healy tossed a big manila envelope on Jesse's desk.

'One shot, behind the right ear, close range. Entrance wound suggests a .38. Slug exited high on the other side, tore out some of her skull. They think they got powder traces. They can't find any on her hands. But the body's deteriorated to the point where they aren't certain. The millimeters and tissue analysis and all, it's in there.'

'Water in her lungs?'

'No,' Healy said. 'She was dead when she went in the water.'

'Could she have shot herself?' Jesse said. 'I mean, was it physically possible given the path of the slug?'

'Yeah, she could have. And the amount of time she was in there could have destroyed the traces on her hands.'

'Drag marks on her?'

Healy shook his head.

'Body's too far gone.'

'So she could have waded out into the lake someplace and shot herself and floated around until we found her. It's a big lake.'

'Gun?' Healy said.

'We got a couple guys from the fire department down there in wet suits,' Jesse said. 'Water's dirty. Hard to see.'

'Even if you find the gun in there,' Healy said, 'why did she want to do it that way?'

'Didn't want anyone to know?'

'Suicides always want people to know,' Healy said. 'That's part of what it's about.'

'True.'

'You find the gun it'll be because the perp threw it in there after her. You know who she is?'

'No. Could they get any prints?'

Healy shook his head.

'Dental?'

'ME charted her teeth,' Healy said.

'So all we have to do is locate a dental chart that matches.'

'In which case you'll know who she is anyway.'

'Missing persons?'

'You know how many kids run away every week?' Healy said.

'Any from Paradise?'

'None reported,' Healy said.

'She could have run away from anywhere and ended up here,' Jesse said.

'She could.'

'You matching the dental charts against the runaways?'

'Sure,' Healy said. 'I got a guy on it.'

'One?'

'You know how things work,' Healy said.

'Slowly,' Jesse said.

'See,' Healy said. 'I knew you'd know.'

'How old was she?'

'Maybe fourteen.'

They were both quiet. The victim's age hung in the room like smoke.

'We'll get on it,' Healy said after a while. 'You come up with anything, let us know.'

'Or vice versa,' Jesse said.

4

Anthony DeAngelo came into Jesse's office leading a male Dalmatian on an improvised leash. The dog was panting, and restless on the leash.

'Got a date?' Jesse said.

'It's a him,' DeAngelo said.

'So?'

'I found him up on the pike running around, you know, like they do when they're lost?'

'Near the donut shop?'

DeAngelo grinned. 'Yeah, how'd you know?'

'I'm an experienced law officer,' Jesse said. 'Molly got any lost dogs?'

'I checked when I came in the station. She says she got two. One's a poodle. One's a Lab.'

Jesse nodded.

'No tags?'

'No collar,' DeAngelo said.

'How'd you get him in the car?' Jesse said.

'Donut.'

'Of course,' Jesse said. 'Where'd you get the nice leash?'

'Lady at the donut shop gave me some twine.'

'You call the dog officer?' Jesse said.

'Valenti? He's working. Don't usually get home till six.'

'Part-time help,' Jesse said. 'Inexpensive and worth it.'

He looked at the dog. Still panting, the dog looked disoriented. He was wagging his tail aimlessly. His ears were flat and his body was a little hunched.

'Okay,' Jesse said, 'put him in one of the cells.'

'Ain't it illegal in this town to domicile dogs and humans in the same space?' DeAngelo said.

'Of course it is,' Jesse said. He looked at DeAngelo without speaking.

'Okay,' DeAngelo said. 'You care which cell?'

'Your choice,' Jesse said. 'And give him some water.'

DeAngelo nodded and led the dog away. Jesse went to the office door and stuck his head out and yelled for Molly Crane.

'Call around to some vets,' he said. 'Describe the dog, see if they know anything about this one.'

'What kind of dog is it?' Molly said.

'Dalmatian. They're not all that common.'

'Male or female?'

'Male,' Jesse said. 'For crissake, you're a cop. You're supposed to be observant.'

'I'm an Irish Catholic girl,' Molly said. 'I don't look at penises.'

'Not even human?'

From the cell block in the back, they could hear the dog begin to howl.

'Especially not human.'

'Always in the dark,' Jesse said.

Molly grinned at him. 'Always. With my eyes tight shut, thinking of Saint Patrick.'

'It's good to be aware of your heritage,' Jesse said. 'Tell Suit I want to talk to him.'

The dog's howling was now steady.

Molly smiled at him. 'Dog's lonely,' she said.

'Ain't we all,' Jesse said.

'Not the way I hear it,' Molly said and went out.

Jesse watched her as she went. She was small and in shape. The blue uniform fit her well. The service pistol looked too large. He knew she was sensual: the way her eyes were. The way she stood. The way she walked. He knew. And she knew he knew.

'There's a dog in cell number one,' Simpson said when he came in.

'Got him for soliciting,' Jesse said.

Simpson hesitated. Jesse said everything in the same sort of serious way, and Simpson was often uncertain if Jesse was kidding. But you couldn't arrest a dog. He laughed.

'He got a lawyer?' Simpson said.

The dog howled.

'I think he'll cop a plea,' Jesse said.

'Yeah,' Simpson said. 'He's already starting to sing.'

'You want to make some overtime?' Jesse said.

'Sure.'

'Go out to the lake where we found the girl, and walk the perimeter. Take Eddie Cox with you. See what you can find.'

'We looking for anything special?'

'A clue would be good.'

'Such as?'

'Anything that looks like a clue,' Jesse said. 'Anything that doesn't belong. That's out of place. That might have once belonged to a teenaged girl. Or a murderer. Or Lillian Gish, for that matter. Whatever you see.'

'Who's Lillian Whatsis?'

'Forget Lillian,' Jesse said. 'Go look.'

'It's a big lake,' Simpson said.

'Take your time. When in doubt, assume it's a clue.'

'I'll call Eddie,' Simpson said.

He stood, hitched his gunbelt a little, and walked from the room. A man on a mission. When he was alone, Jesse sat for a moment listening to the dog howl. Then he got up and found a roll of crime scene tape and cut off a length and went down to the cell block. The dog stopped howling the minute he saw Jesse. His tail wagged hesitantly. Jesse opened the door and went in.

'We can improve your accommodations,' Jesse said to the dog. 'You can stay with the chief of police himself.'

He looped the length of plastic tape around the dog's neck and led the dog back down the corridor to his office.

5

The dog was sleeping behind Jesse's desk. When Jenn came into Jesse's office at twenty minutes past five, the dog raised his head and growled at her. Jenn stopped short.

'I know you've gone out with some dogs since we broke up,' Jenn said, 'but right in the office?'

'His name's Deputy,' Jesse said.

'His?'

'We're just friends,' Jesse said.

'Well, can you leave your friend long enough to go to dinner with me?'

'I feel like I ought to bring him,' Jesse said.

'For God's sake,' Jenn said. 'Don't you have a dog officer in this town?'

'Yeah. Bob Valenti. Part-time guy.'

'Well, call him up, have him take the dog to the kennel or the pound or whatever you call it.'

'He howls when I leave him,' Jesse said.

Jenn squatted in front of the dog. Given how tight Jenn wore her pants, Jesse thought it was no small thing. But she did it easily, though it made her pants pull tighter over the curve of her butt.

'Does he bite?'

'I don't know,' Jesse said. 'He's only been here a couple of hours.'

Jenn put her hand out. *Women*, Jesse thought, *squat much more gracefully than men.*

'Clench your fist,' Jesse said. 'It makes it harder for him to bite your hand.'

'Jesus,' Jenn said and jerked her hand back.

The dog kept his head up, looking at her. She made a fist and put it toward the dog's nose very carefully. The dog sniffed at her fist carefully, and thumped the floor with his tail a couple of times.

'I think he likes me,' Jenn said.

'Probably,' Jesse said.

'If we take him with us, won't he howl when we leave him in the car?'

'We could eat in the car,' Jesse said.

Jenn stared at him.

Finally she said, 'Jesse, haven't you killed several people?'

Jesse nodded.

'And yet you can't leave a stray dog to have dinner with your ex-wife who, I guess, still loves you, and whom I believe you still love, for fear that the dog will be unhappy?'

Jesse nodded.

'What would we eat in the car?' Jenn said.

'Pizza?'

'Split three ways?' Jenn said.

'I guess.'

'And maybe a six-pack?'

'Sure,' Jesse said.

'Glad I dressed up,' Jenn said.

Jesse stood. The dog stood as soon as Jesse did.

'We're glad, too,' Jesse said.

In Jesse's car, the dog sat in the backseat. And in the parking lot of Paradise Pizza, the dog rested his head on the back of Jenn's seat while Jesse and Jenn ate a pizza with green peppers and mushrooms and drank beer from the can.

'Can I give him my pizza crust?' Jenn said.

'I think he likes those,' Jesse said.

Jenn offered a crust to the dog. He ate it and swallowed and waited. Jesse opened a second can of beer. *This is the last one. For God's sake don't get drunk in front of her.*

'How are you?' Jesse said.

'I'm fine, Jesse.'

'I watch you do the weather almost every night.'

'Good.'

'Do you actually know what a low-pressure system is?' Jesse said.

Jenn smiled. She gave the dog another crust.

'No, but I'm getting very good at pretending I'm pointing at a real weather map.'

'Behind the scenes,' Jesse said, 'show biz just isn't pretty.'

'No.'

'You still dating the anchorman?'

Jenn smiled. 'No. I hate to date people cuter than I am.'

Jesse sipped a little beer. *Easy*, he thought. *Easy does it.* He spoke as casually as he could.

'So who you dating these days?'

'You, for one,' Jenn said.

'And?'

'Others,' Jenn said.

'Like who?'

'Like guys,' Jenn said. 'Why do you need to ask? What's the point?'

'I don't know.'

'It's just the kind of question that pushes me away,' Jenn said.

He thought of saying that it was, probably, however distorted, a form of love. But he didn't. It would only make them argue.

'It's the kind of possessive question that drove me away in the first place,' Jenn said.

'When we were married it was probably more appropriate,' Jesse said.

Jenn was silent. Then he could see a little of the tension go out of her shoulders.

'Yes,' she said. 'It probably was.'

His beer was gone. Jesse didn't even recall drinking it. He felt swollen with sadness and desire. He opened a third can. Jenn patted his right thigh.

'We're still here,' Jenn said.

From the backseat the dog nosed the back of Jenn's neck, looking for another crust.

'We are,' Jesse said.

6

After Jenn left, Jesse drank four scotch and sodas before bed. In the morning, at 7:15, sitting in his office, he felt a little shaky, and a little guilty. He tried coffee, but the coffee didn't help either one. At ten past nine a woman who introduced herself as Miriam Lowell showed up wearing a lavender warm-up suit and white sneakers. She was also wearing big gold hoop earrings, and rings on four fingers, and a gold necklace with some sort of big medallion on it.

'I believe you have my dog,' she said.

The dog was very pleased. He had jumped up and put his forepaws against the owner's stomach and was lapping her face. Miriam Lowell squinched up her face and took it for a little while. Then she put his collar on him and hooked his leash. The dog capered a little bit. 'His name is Baron,' she said.

'We've been calling him Deputy,' Jesse said.

'Deputy?'

'Like in Deputy Dawg?' Jesse said.

The woman appeared to see no logic in that.

'He was here all the time?' she said.

'Since yesterday,' Jesse said. 'Last night he stayed with me.'

'At your home?'

'Yes.'

'I would think,' she said, 'that the police department would have made a more successful attempt to bring him to his rightful home.'

'He was roaming around on the pike with no license,' Jesse said. 'We asked him where he lived, and he refused to answer.'

'Well,' the woman said. 'There's no need to be snippy.'

'Maybe a little snippy,' Jesse said.

He bent over and the dog licked his face. Jesse patted him. The woman hesitated for a moment, then turned and marched out with her dog.

'No trouble at all,' Jesse said in the empty room. 'Glad we could help.'

Then he smiled to himself and picked up Deputy's water dish and emptied it in the sink. The coffee tasted bitter. He dumped that in the sink too, and mixed up some Alka-Seltzer and drank it. At least Jenn didn't know he'd gotten drunk. With her he'd been able to stop without finishing the third beer. He always liked leaving a drink unfinished. It made him feel that he had no drinking problem.

Jesse heard someone yelling from the holding cells. After it had gone on for a while, Jesse yelled out his office door for Molly Crane. She came into the office.

'Unhappy prisoner?' Jesse said.

'Name's Bellino,' Molly said. 'Perkins and DeAngelo arrested him last night up at The Sevens.'

'Drunk and disorderly?'

'How'd you guess?'

'He still drunk?'

'I don't think so. I think he's just making a lot of noise to show how dangerous he is. You want to read the arrest report?'

Jesse nodded. Molly went out and came back with the report. Jesse read it. The yelling from the cell block seemed to intensify.

When he was through reading the report, Jesse tossed it on his desk, stood, took off his gun, put it in his desk drawer and locked the drawer.

'You going to talk with him?' Molly said.

'I am.'

'He's a big guy,' Molly said.

'I hate noise,' Jesse said.

He walked down the corridor to the holding cells, and stopped in front of the first cell. Inside the cell was a fat, strong-looking man with shoulder-length dark hair.

'Got a hangover?' Jesse said.

'I'm going to pull the fucking door off its fucking hinges you don't let me out of here,' the fat man said.

'I'll take that as a yes.'

Jesse unlocked the cell door and walked in and let it click shut behind him.

'I'm going out,' Bellino said.

'You have been arrested,' Jesse said. 'You're going to have to make a court appearance.'

'Fuckers pepper-sprayed me,' Bellino said.

'Meanwhile,' Jesse said. 'I want you to quiet down.'

'Fuck you,' Bellino said.

'You want a lawyer yet?' Jesse said.

'Fuck you,' Bellino said.

'I'll take that as a no,' Jesse said.

'I ought to kick your fucking ass,' Bellino said.

'You got drunk,' Jesse said, 'and made an asshole of yourself. And now you're trying to pretend you didn't.'

'Guy gave me shit,' Bellino said.

'Guy you punched out?' Jesse said.

'Yeah. I'm supposed to take shit from some asshole don't even live here? I'm supposed to let some small-town jerkoff cops blindside me with pepper spray?'

'Why not?'

'I don't take shit,' Bellino said.

'We all take shit,' Jesse said. 'And we all like to pretend we don't.'

'You think I'm pretending?'

'Nobody likes to face up to being a stupid drunk,' Jesse said.

'You calling me stupid?'

'Sure,' Jesse said. 'Everybody's stupid when they drink.'

'You little fuck,' Bellino said, and shoved Jesse.

Jesse kneed him in the groin. As Bellino flinched, his head lowered and Jesse took a left handful of his hair and pulled Bellino forward past him and caught Bellino's wrist with his right hand and turned Bellino's arm up behind Bellino's back. He ran Bellino across the small cell and banged him face first up against the cell wall and held him there. Bellino was gasping for air. Jesse held him against the wall another minute while the hot haze of his anger seeped back into him and dissipated. When Jesse let Bellino go, Bellino staggered to the bunk along the other wall of the cell and sank onto it, his breath rasping in and out.

'I want you to be quiet,' Jesse said. 'Later this morning someone will take you over to Peabody and you'll appear before a magistrate and pay a fine and go home ... quietly.'

Bellino nodded.

'Everybody's a jerk sometimes,' Jesse said.

'You hadn't kicked me in the balls ...' Bellino said.

'But I did,' Jesse said. 'And might again.'

'Cops ain't supposed to hit somebody they arrested.'

Jesse smiled at him. 'That's correct,' Jesse said.

He turned and left the cell and locked the door.

7

It was a bright summer morning. Jesse was feeling good. *Every day you don't have a hangover is a good day.* He pulled the unmarked Ford off of Summer Street up onto Morton Drive. At the end of the drive, parked on a shoulder near the lake, was a Paradise cruiser. Suitcase Simpson was leaning on it with his arms folded. As Jesse approached, he held up a clear plastic evidence bag.

'Found this about a half mile that way,' Simpson said. 'Right near the water. Eddie's still down there, but I thought you should see this.'

Jesse put out his hand. Simpson gave him the bag. In it was a densely engraved ring with a big blue stone. There was a broken length of gold chain tangled around the ring.

'School ring,' Jesse said.

'That's my guess,' Simpson said. 'I didn't want to handle it more than I had to so I dropped it right into the bag as soon as I found it.'

'The chain with it?'

'Looped through, just like that,' Simpson said.

Jesse opened the evidence bag and took out the ring.

'What about prints?' Simpson said.

'No chance,' Jesse said. 'Look at the surface.'

'Maybe the stone, though.'

Jesse smiled. 'I won't touch the stone.'

Jesse looked at the ring. Engraved around the blue stone were the words SWAMPSCOTT HIGH SCHOOL, 2000. Jesse tried it on. It was too big for him.

'Well, I guess it wasn't hers,' Simpson said. 'If it's too big for you.'

'That's what the chain is for,' Jesse said. 'Didn't the girls in your high school do that? Wear the boyfriend's ring on a chain around their neck?'

'Sometimes,' Simpson said. 'So you think it might be hers?'

'Doesn't do us any good to think it's not,' Jesse said. 'Show me where you found it.'

It was hot, and still. As they walked down through tall grass and short bushes toward the edge of the lake, Jesse could smell the mud where the shore and water met. Ahead, Eddie Cox was moving along the edge of the shore, head down, looking at the ground. The back of his blue uniform shirt was dark with sweat.

'Right over here,' Simpson said.

Cox looked up and turned back and joined them.

'You think it's something, Jesse?' Cox said.

'Maybe.'

'We found it right here,' Simpson said. 'It was snagged on this little bush.'

Jesse squatted on his heels, looking at the bush and the ground around it.

'When did it rain last?' Jesse said.

'Tuesday,' Simpson said. 'I remember, the Sox game got washed out.'

Jesse kept looking.

'What are you looking for?' Cox asked.

'She probably weighed a hundred, hundred and twenty. That's a lot of dead weight to carry, unless you're in pretty good shape.'

'So you figure he dragged her?'

'He's probably not too calm while he's dragging her. When the ring around her neck snagged, he just tugged her loose and kept dragging.'

Jesse continued to sit on his heels and look around him.

'There's a little cul-de-sac up the hill,' Jesse said. 'Off Newbury Street. DPW uses it to pile sand for the winter.'

'Kids go in there to smoke dope,' Simpson said.

'And make out,' Cox said.

'Smoke and moke,' Simpson said. He reddened a little, taking pleasure in his wit.

'The perfect combo,' Jesse said.

He stood and began to walk up the hill toward the cul-de-sac. Cox and Simpson followed. They wanted to watch Jesse. He'd been a homicide cop. L.A., where there were murders all the time. Main Street bordered the lake at right angles to Morton Drive. By the time he reached the top of the hill he was nearly a mile from his car. He stood in the cul-de-sac and looked back down toward the place where they had found the ring. He was talking aloud as much to himself as to Simpson and Cox.

'It's dark, and darker in here. Guy pulls in. She's probably dead. He's probably got her in the trunk.'

As he talked, Jesse walked through the ideas. Maybe in the replay there'd be something to notice.

'Takes her out of the trunk. Probably can't pick her up. People see it in the movies all the time. But in fact, a hundred and twenty pounds of dead weight is more than most guys can handle. So he drags her out. Might have her wrapped up. Might not. But there should be blood.'

Jesse squatted again and looked at the gravel surface of the cul-de-sac.

'It was a big rain,' Simpson said.

Jesse nodded. Jesse knew how much it had rained Tuesday night. But Simpson was trying to be helpful and Jesse didn't want to discourage him.

'So if there was some, it's been washed away,' Jesse said. He stood and imagined dragging the girl's body from the trunk and along the ground.

'Gets her out and arranged, then starts to drag her. Probably by the arms, unless he had rope or something. And he drags her backwards down the hill. It'll be slow going.' Jesse began to back down the hill.

'But there is a sort of path,' Jesse said. 'Kids probably bring beer in, drink it by the lake.'

He paused, looking at a broken branch on one of the short bushes. He pulled it toward him a little and looked at it.

'Leaves are still green.'

'So it hasn't been broken very long,' Simpson said.

Farther down the slope was a pair of branches, barely above ground level, that had been broken as well.

'He gets to the lake,' Jesse said. 'And he puts her in. Does he just leave her there?'

'If he didn't care about her being found, he wouldn't have gone to all this trouble,' Simpson said.

'So he wanted her to sink,' Cox said.

'But not right here,' Jesse said. 'First kid came down here with a Miller Lite would spot her.'

'So he had to drag her out a ways,' Simpson said.

He was excited. It was like a real murder investigation.

'She'd have dragged easier in the water,' Jesse said.

He stepped into the lake. It was barely knee high. It deepened only gradually as he waded out. He stopped when the water reached his crotch.

'If he wanted her to sink,' Simpson said from the shore, 'he'd have weighted her.'

'But not on shore,' Jesse said. 'It would have made dragging her that much harder. He wouldn't want to weight her until he got her deep enough to let her sink.'

'I read the ME's report,' Simpson said. ' 'Fore I came out here to sweep the place. There's no sign of any weight being attached.'

'How many shoes she have on?' Jesse said. 'When we found her?'

'Shoes? One.'

'What if he tied the weight around an ankle,' Jesse said. 'And after it was in the water for a while the body began to decompose and become more buoyant at the same time it was becoming less, ah, cohesive, and the rope dragged off her ankle and took a shoe with it?'

'So, the weight and the rope should be in the water around here.'

'It should,' Jesse said.

8

Jesse could hear the music from beyond the curve. As he came around the curve he could barely squeeze his own car between the cars parked on both sides of the street. He could see the blue light revolving on the roof of Arthur Angstrom's cruiser parked in the driveway of a big, sprawling Victorian house that sat at the top of a rolling lawn. Angstrom stood beside the cruiser talking to a short man with a dark tan. The man was partially bald. His remaining hair was gray and hung to his shoulders.

'You're Chief Stone?' the man said.

'Yes.'

'I'm Norman Shaw.'

'I know.'

Shaw looked gratified. 'Good,' he said. 'Your officer here appears to think there's a crime being committed here.'

Shaw's eyes were bloodshot, and beneath the tan on his face was a web of broken veins. He was wearing shorts and a white oxford shirt with the tails out. His legs were tan and skinny and nearly hairless. He wasn't fat, but he had an assertive belly that pushed against the shirt.

'Actually he's not my officer,' Jesse said. 'He's yours. He works for the town.'

'Casuistry aside,' Shaw said, 'I like to talk with the man in charge.'

'That would be me,' Jesse said.

'Young for the job,' Shaw said.

'I'm aging fast, though.'

'Well, I am sure you're old enough to explain to this officer …'

'Angstrom,' Jesse said. 'Officer Angstrom.'

'I'm sure you can explain to him that Party Patrol is not the best use a policeman can make of his time.'

'You had a complaint?' Jesse said to Arthur.

'Noise,' Angstrom said. 'Obstructing access. Drunk and disorderly. Public lewdness. Littering. Urinating on a private lawn.'

'Punishable by death?' Shaw said. 'It's a party, for God's sake. The Lieutenant Governor is here. Michael DeSisto came all the way from Stockbridge. There are state reps. A congressman. My attorney. Do I have to get my attorney down here?'

'Chills run up and down my spine,' Jesse said. 'You'll have to move some cars.' He turned to Angstrom. 'You got the names of the complainants?'

'Yep.'

'Will they point out the culprits?'

'They say so.'

'Move cars?' Shaw said. 'You expect me to go from person to person asking if they own the fucking blue Mercedes or the black Saab?'

'Yes.'

'And take all the juice right out of the party?'

'That's not a bad thing,' Jesse said.

'Well, I'm not doing it.'

Jesse shrugged. 'Call Frankie's Tow,' he said to Arthur. 'Have them start hooking up.'

'Tow?'

'Yep.'

'You can't tow all these cars.'

Jesse ignored him. 'Then get John Maguire out here, and Peter Perkins. They're on shift. Have John supervise the towing. You and Peter get the complainants over here and start arresting the guests.'

'For what?'

'Noise,' Jesse said. 'Obstructing access. Drunk and disorderly. Public lewdness. Littering. Urinating on a private lawn.'

'You are going to get yourself in serious trouble,' Shaw said.

His face was flushed under the tan, and he was breathing harshly. 'You have no idea what kind of guest list is here.'

'Gee, maybe we'll make the papers,' Jesse said.

A woman in tight calf-length pants and a glistening silvery tank top came down the lawn carrying a cocktail.

Martini, Jesse thought.

The woman stopped beside Shaw and stood so that she was touching him.

'What's going on, Normy?'

She was taller than Shaw, with straight blond hair worn long. Her breasts pushed hard against the silvery tank top, and the pants fit tight over her thighs. Her features were elegantly proportional. And her teeth were even and perfectly white. Everyone had teeth like that in L.A.

Bonded, Jesse thought.

'These … policemen feel that we are entirely lawless,' Shaw said.

He took the martini from her and drank some and handed her back the glass.

'Oh, pooh,' the woman said and smiled at Jesse. 'Have a drink. Lighten up.'

'No drinks, ma'am.'

'Oh my,' she said, 'so solemn. I'm Joni Shaw.'

She put out her hand to Jesse. She was quick. She had already figured out who was in charge. Jesse didn't shake hands.

'Jesse Stone,' he said.

She smiled. The smile was very strong. Jesse could feel it.

'And do you really want to ruin our party? It's Normy's annual publication party.'

'We don't want to ruin your party,' Jesse said. 'But cars need to be moved. Behavior needs to be modified.'

'Every year when his new novel comes out, we throw this huge bash. Normy's agent is here. There are film people. Publishing people. Politicians. The Lieutenant Governor is here.'

'Mr. Shaw mentioned the Lieutenant Governor,' Jesse said. 'Get on the radio, Arthur. Call the tow company.'

Angstrom slid into his car and started his call.

'We'll move the cars,' Joni Shaw said.

'And keep people from wandering into the neighbors' yards?'

'I'll do my best.'

'I'm going to have your job,' Shaw said.

'Probably not,' Jesse said.

He smiled at Joni Shaw. She smiled back at him.

9

'They moved the cars,' Angstrom said as he came into Jesse's office. 'And she went around and told people to cool it.'

'You leave Perkins there?'

'Him and John,' Angstrom said. 'I'm sorry I had to drag you out there.'

'It's why I get the big bucks, Arthur.'

'My wife wore pants as tight as Mrs. Shaw I wouldn't let her out in public,' Angstrom said. 'How the fuck she get them on?'

'She's probably a strong-willed woman,' Jesse said.

'What's casuistry mean?' Arthur said.

'I have no idea,' Jesse said.

Suitcase came into the office with Doc Lane. He was carrying a big evidence bag, which he held up as if he'd caught a record-breaking fish. Doc had a cinder block in each hand, which he set on the floor by Jesse's desk.

'Doc found it,' Simpson said.

'Rope and shoe?'

'Tied to a couple of cinder blocks,' Doc said.

He was a rangy, weathered guy who fished, and tended bar at night, and did the diving for the police when there was any to do.

'Any gun?'

'None that I could find,' Doc said. 'The bottom is muck, Jesse. Gun could be under ten feet of it, if it's in there at all.'

Jesse looked at the rope. It was the kind that you buy in fifty-foot lengths at lumber yards, about the size of clothesline, but made of nylon. When you cut it, you needed to burn the ends, so the rope wouldn't unravel.

'The ends are frayed,' Jesse said.

'Two of them are mine,' Doc said. 'I had to cut it loose from the cinder blocks.'

'I see that. The other ends are starting to unravel. Means he probably cut it at the time he used it, and didn't have time to melt the cut end.'

'Or he was in the water,' Simpson said, 'and the matches were wet.'

There was one small shoe tangled in the rope.

'Looks like the one she was wearing,' Jesse said. 'We'll get a size match.'

It was the first time either Simpson or Angstrom had seen one of the shoes. Neither had looked at her when she came out of the water.

'Penny loafer,' Angstrom said. 'I got three daughters and none of them had any penny loafers.'

'A retro girl,' Jesse said.

'You need me anymore, Jesse?' Doc said.

'No. Thank you. Send me a bill, and I'll buck it over to the town clerk.'

Doc left. Jesse stood and went around his desk and squatted on his heels and looked at the cinder blocks. They were still damp.

'New,' Jesse said. 'Arthur, now that you've brought law and order to Paradise Neck, go around to hardware stores and lumber yards and see if anyone bought two cinder blocks and some nylon rope in the last month or so.'

'In what area?'

'North shore,' Jesse said. 'To start.'

'Lot of people buy rope and cinder block.'

'Yeah, but how many buy two cinder blocks and some rope at the same time?'

'You think the guy was that stupid?' Simpson said.

'Maybe. And maybe he used a credit card,' Jesse said.

'That would be amazingly stupid,' Simpson said.

'We can hope,' Jesse said.

10

Jesse wasn't in uniform when he walked into Swampscott High School. He wore jeans and a blue blazer and a white shirt with the collar open. Summer school was in session and kids with bad grades, or bad attitudes, or overzealous parents, were in their classrooms. Jesse felt the old feeling as he walked along the empty corridor. He had always disliked school. Had always thought it full of cant and nonsense. And in his adulthood, he was sometimes startled at how early in life he'd been right.

In the outer office, at her desk, behind her computer, guarding the principal's gate, was a portly woman with a tight gray perm and a long blue dress. She looked at Jesse as if he'd just been loitering in the hall.

'Jesse Stone?' he said. 'For Lilly Summers?'

'Do you have an appointment with Doctor Summers?' the guardian said. She underscored the 'Doctor.'

'I do.'

'Regarding what?'

Jesse took out his badge holder and flipped it open. The guardian craned her neck at it as if it were too small to see.

'Are you with the police?' she said.

'I am.'

'Well, why didn't you say so?'

'I don't know.'

'Wait here.'

Jesse smiled as the guardian lumbered into the principal's office. *She'll keep me waiting longer than she needs to*, he thought. *Make sure I know that* Dr. *Summers is important*. It took almost five minutes for the guardian to deliver the fact of Jesse's presence and for *Dr.* Summers to agree that, in fact, Stone had an appointment. Finally the guardian came out and left Dr. Summers's door open and frowned at Jesse and stood aside. Given her heft, she had to stand a good distance aside for Jesse to get by.

Inside, Dr. Summers stood and put out her hand. She was a slender woman with a young face and silver hair. Jesse wondered if she was older than she looked, or if her silver hair was premature. He decided she was young, and the hair made her look distinguished. If she were older she'd color her hair to look younger.

'Jesse Stone,' he said.

'Sit down, Mr. Stone,' she said. 'You're with the Paradise Police?'

'Yes.'

'And it's something ...' She looked distressed. 'About a murder?'

He noticed she wore no wedding ring. It meant less than it once might have, Jesse knew. A lot of married women, especially married professional women, no longer wore wedding bands.

'Yes,' Jesse said. 'Last week we found the body of a young woman who'd been dead for several weeks, in a lake in Paradise.'

'How awful.'

'Especially for her,' Jesse said. 'She had been shot in the head.'

'Someone killed her?'

'Yes. On a chain around her neck was a Swampscott High School ring, class of two thousand.'

Jesse took the ring out and placed it on the desk in front of Dr. Summers. Dr. Summers was wearing a black linen suit and a crimson shirt. As she shifted in her chair to look at the ring, Jesse saw that the suit fit her very well. She was wearing a nice perfume, too.

'My God,' she said.

Jesse nodded.

'Is there a way to know whose ring this is?' Jesse said.

'From the size,' Dr. Summers said, 'I assume it was a young man.'

'And a member of the class of two thousand.'

'Yes.'

'Any way to know which one?'

'We graduated a hundred and thirteen young men in June,' Dr. Summers said.

She crossed her legs. Jesse noticed that her legs looked good.

'Do you have any young women from the school that are missing?'

'None that I know of. It is, of course, summer. I'd have no way to know once school ended.'

'And the victim doesn't have to be from your school,' Jesse said. 'Does every graduating senior get a ring automatically?'

'No. They have to be ordered. And some students don't bother.'

'To show you they don't like the school,' Jesse said.

'I imagine so,' Dr. Summers said. 'They are often among the more disaffected.'

'Not a bad thing,' Jesse said.

'Disaffection? No, not at all. Were you disaffected, Chief Stone?'

'You bet,' Jesse said. 'Do you have a record of the orders?'

'No. We order from a company called C. C. Benjamin, in Boston. Did you attend college?'

'No,' Jesse said. 'I went from high school to a minor-league baseball team.'

'Really? Did you ever play major-league baseball?'

'No. I was a shortstop. Got as far as Albuquerque and tore up my shoulder.'

'The one you throw with?'

'Yes.'

'That would be a bad injury for a shortstop.'

'Fatal,' Jesse said. 'You follow baseball, Dr. Summers?'

'Lilly,' she said. 'Yes, very closely.'

'Did your husband play?'

She smiled at him. 'There is no husband, Chief Stone.'

Jesse smiled back at her.

'Jesse,' he said.

They looked at each other silently for a moment, and just as he realized suddenly that she was good-looking, he understood suddenly that she was sexual. Her eyes. The way she moved. The way she held herself.

'How will you identify her?' Lilly said.

'We'll ask everyone who ordered a class ring to account for theirs.'

'And if they can't?'

'It narrows the list. Then we ask around as to which of these guys had a girlfriend, and what was her name, and see if she's missing.'

'Labor intensive,' Lilly said.

'It is,' Jesse said.

'Is it usually this laborious?' Lilly said.

'No, usually you got a pretty good idea that it was the husband, or Uncle Harry or whatever, and you set out to prove

33

it. Murder is fairly unusual anyway, especially in a town like Paradise. Most of it is drunk driving and lost dogs and kids smoking dope in the town cemetery. But here we don't even know who the victim was yet.'

'And there's no missing-person's report that would be her?'

'No.'

'Isn't that unusual?'

'Yes.'

Lilly crossed her legs the other way. Jesse waited.

'How did you go from shortstop to policeman, Jesse?'

'My father was a cop,' Jesse said. 'In Tucson. When I couldn't play ball anymore, it seemed like the other thing I might know how to do.'

'And how did you end up in Paradise?'

'I was a cop in L.A. I got fired for being a drunk. And my marriage broke up. And I figured I'd try to start over as far from L.A. as I could.'

'Are you still drinking?'

'Mostly not,' Jesse said.

'Was that why your marriage broke up?'

'No,' Jesse said. 'It didn't help the marriage, and the marriage didn't help it. But there were other things.'

'There always are, aren't there.'

'You've been divorced?'

'Twice.'

'Are you seeing anyone?'

'No.'

Jesse was quiet for a time, sitting motionless in the straight-backed high school chair.

'Well,' he said finally. 'Hello.'

11

They had lost 8 to 5. The field lights had been turned off and they were in the parking lot drinking beer in the semidarkness.

'I was a month out of high school,' Jesse said. 'And we were playing in Danville.'

It was Jesse's turn to buy the beer. It was in a green plastic cooler, buried in ice, in the back of Jesse's Explorer. The rear door of the Explorer was up. Jesse's glove was in the back of the truck, too, and the bases, and a green canvas bag with bat handles sticking out.

'Had a third baseman, an old guy, twenty-eight probably, ancient to be playing at that level. He was a career minor leaguer, and knew it, and played I think because he sort of didn't know what else to do.'

The winning team was across the parking lot gathered around their beer cooler like hunters at a campfire. There was no hostility, but there wasn't much interchange. After a game you clustered with your team.

'Anyway, in the first inning there's two outs, nobody on and their three hitter pops up a goddamned rainmaker to the left side. We were playing in a damn cow pasture and the lights were set too low and the sucker went up out of sight.'

The smell of the lake was with them in the slow-deepening purple of the evening, and a few early explorers had arrived in advance of the inevitable insect swarm that would, as it always did, eventually force them to give it up and go back to the ordinary light of their homes.

'I'm looking up trying to find it when it comes back into the light, and the third baseman says, 'You got it, kid.' And everybody trots off the field while I'm weaving around out there looking for the ball.'

Everyone listened to Jesse quietly. They were men to whom such stories mattered. Men who would know why the story was funny. Men who could imagine the scared kid alone in the middle of the diamond looking up into the night for his first professional pop-up.

'You catch it?' someone said.

The younger guys listened most closely. Kids who would fall asleep in class, listening to Jesse talk about life in the minors, as if he were Socrates.

'Barely,' Jesse said.

Everyone laughed. They were happy with the story. They all knew that the better you were, the more you talked about your failures. Jesse was clearly the best player in the league, maybe good enough to have played in the majors if he hadn't got hurt.

'You win the game?' someone asked.

'Don't know. But I went two for four.'

Everyone laughed again. Jesse had been there. They could laugh with him at the pretense that players cared only about winning. You played ball, you knew better.

Jesse finished his beer. One more wouldn't hurt. It was Lite beer anyway. You could drink a lot of Lite beer before you got drunk enough to show it. He plunged his hand into the ice-filled cooler and rummaged out another can. It had a round solid feel to it, cold in his hand.

'You have a lot of groupies in the minors, Jess?'

'Not enough,' Jesse said.

'When I was playing football,' someone said, 'we'd go into some town for an away game, they'd be waiting outside the visitors' locker room.'

'You score?'

'During the game or after?'

They all laughed.

'After.'

'A lot more than during,' the football player said.

'What about AIDS?'

'It was before AIDS,' the football player said.

It was dark now. The kind of thick summer darkness that feels soft. Oddly the bugs hadn't found them yet in thick enough quantity to drive them home.

'I remember playing hockey in Helsinki,' somebody said. 'Outdoor rink. Was so fucking cold the puck froze. One of our guys tees up a big slap shot from the blue line and the goddamned puck shatters.'

People began to drift home. To wives. And children. And late suppers. And living rooms lit by the glow of a large-screen television.

'You find out who killed that girl yet, Jesse?'

'Not yet,' Jesse said. 'But I went three for three tonight.'

12

'I got twelve names,' Jesse said to Lilly Summers. 'Kids gave their class rings to a girl.'

'Makes last year's class seem embarrassingly unromantic,' Lilly said.

'Embarrassingly,' Jesse said. 'Seven of these kids can account for their girlfriends' whereabouts, and we've verified it.'

'Which leaves you five.'

'Four of them are supposed to be at summer homes with their parents, but we haven't been able to reach them yet. One boy doesn't know where she is.'

'And her parents?'

'Kid didn't know anything about her parents,' Jesse said.

'How could that be?' Lilly said. 'What are the names?'

'Boyfriend's name is William Royce,' Jesse said.

Lilly smiled. 'Hooker,' she said.

'And the girlfriend is Elinor Bishop.'

'Oh dear,' Lilly said.

'You know them.'

'Yes, of course.'

'You have an address for her?'

'She called herself Billie. Yes, I have her address.'

'Could you talk to me,' Jesse said, 'about Hooker and Billie?'

'How long do you have?'

'If it's a longish story we could do it over lunch.'

Lilly smiled. She was wearing a pale yellow silk dress today. 'What a very good idea,' she said.

37

It was low tide. They sat in a small restaurant that looked out over Fisherman's Beach at the gunmetal Atlantic rolling stolidly in onto the shiny sand. The ocean smell was strong. Even if you didn't look at it, it was there in that mysterious way that the sea asserts itself.

'I hope it's not Billie,' Lilly said.

'It's going to be somebody,' Jesse said.

They ordered iced tea and looked at their menus. Lilly ordered a house salad, dressing on the side. Jesse had a tuna fish sandwich.

'Hooker Royce,' Lilly said, 'is our All-American. Honor roll since first grade. Three sports, captain in all of them. All-state in football. Scholarship to Yale.'

'And he's handsome and self-effacing,' Jesse said.

'How did you know?'

'They're always self-effacing and handsome.'

'All of them?'

'All the small-school heroes, it's part of the heroism. The expectations of the town force it upon them.'

'Even the handsome?'

'Might be sort of circular. Probably wouldn't be the town hero if he were ugly.'

'Even if he were just as good?' Lilly said.

'Maybe,' Jesse said.

'Well, that's cynical.'

'Or observant.'

She smiled at him. 'Being observant would make you cynical,' Lilly said. 'Wouldn't it?'

'You seem observant,' Jesse said.

'I try.'

'But you don't seem cynical.'

'I'm in the hope business,' Lilly said.

'Education?'

'Yes.'

'You think you might be saving them?'

'I have to think so, or hope so,' Lilly said. 'Otherwise what

38

have I done with my life?'

Jesse sipped his iced tea and looked at her. Lilly's eyes were almond shaped and dark brown, maybe black. Her skin was smooth. She wore quite a bit of makeup, but carefully.

'What about Billie?' Jesse said.

Lilly breathed deeply through her nose. It made her chest move.

'Billie Bishop,' she said.

Jesse was quiet. Lilly shook her head gently.

'Billie was …' She stopped to think about it. 'Billie was our town pump,' she said.

'Don't beat around the bush,' Jesse said.

'I know. It's a terrible thing to say, isn't it?'

'We used to say it when I was a kid,' Jesse said.

'We all did,' Lilly said. 'It says everything and nothing.'

Jesse nodded. There were potato chips with his sandwich. Jesse ate one.

'I'm more interested in everything,' he said.

'Yes.'

Jesse looked at the ocean. It was uninterrupted here, stretching to Spain. In Jesse's imagination, the Atlantic was a gray ocean. The Pacific had been blue.

'Teachers hear things, and they gossip.'

'I'm shocked,' Jesse said.

Lilly smiled. 'Billie,' she said, 'was probably what we would have called, in less enlightened times, a nymphomaniac.'

Jesse smiled. 'Not a bad thing in a woman,' he said.

Lilly looked at him thoughtfully.

'Sexuality is not a bad thing in a woman,' she said.

'It certainly isn't.'

'But frequent indiscriminate sex probably is,' Lilly said. 'However outmoded the phrase, it at least served to identify sexuality rooted in something wrong.'

'So does "town pump."'

'Yes.'

'And there's something wrong with Billie?'

'I think so. A school principal knows very little about the souls of her students.'

Jesse nodded.

'But I do know her external circumstances.'

Jesse waited.

'She is not a discipline problem in the sense of an angry rebellious teenager that we all think of in this context....'

Lilly stopped suddenly and looked at Jesse again. Jesse waited.

'I don't know if I should be talking to you like this.'

'It's okay,' Jesse said. 'I'm the police.'

'You are not even one of our police,' she said.

'True.'

'There's something so quiet about you.'

Jesse nodded.

'And it's charming in a way I don't exactly understand,' Lilly said.

'Good,' Jesse said.

'That it's charming, or that I don't understand?'

'That I have your attention,' Jesse said.

They were silent.

'Yes, you do,' Lilly said finally.

Jesse smiled at her. She smiled back. Then she let her breath out audibly.

'Billie comes from a home,' she said, 'that would be officially classified as "good."'

'By which we normally mean two parents and some money.'

Lilly nodded.

'Anything wrong with the parents?'

'Except that their daughter is a mess?' Lilly said. 'I don't know. I've never met them.'

'Any of her teachers know them?'

'They were invited to come in and discuss their daughter's problems several times. But they never did.'

'Siblings?' Jesse said.

'Her older sister graduated this school with honors. There is, I believe, a younger girl as well.'

'In school here?'

'No. Still in middle school, I think.'

'So aside from a tendency toward frequent indiscriminate sex, what kind of mess is she?'

'She failed a number of courses, which is, as you may know, in today's educational climate, not easy.'

'She dumb?'

'No. Extremely passive. Apathetic. She never speaks in class. Between classes she didn't interact with other students.'

'Didn't?'

'Excuse me?'

'You've been talking about her in the present tense until you said she *didn't* interact. Why the tense change?'

'Hooker,' Lilly said.

'She interacted with Hooker?'

'Intensely,' Lilly said. 'Have you met him?'

'No, one of the other cops talked to him on the phone.'

'He's a lovely boy,' Lilly said.

'So how did the school hero end up with the town pump?' Jesse said.

'I don't know,' Lilly said.

'Maybe it was influenced by the nymphomania.'

'There's that cynical thing again,' Lilly said.

'You have any idea where Billie might be now?'

Lilly shook her head. They both stared out the window for a time at the ocean, always in motion, going nowhere.

'If she's missing, wouldn't her parents have reported her missing?'

'You'd think so,' Jesse said.

'But they haven't?'

'Not that I can find out. Swampscott cops have nothing.'

'Do you think the girl in the lake is Billie?' Lilly said.

'Be my guess,' Jesse said.

13

On Saturday morning, a Swampscott patrolman named Antonelli took Jesse to visit Billie Bishop's parents. The Bishops lived on Garland Terrace, off Humphrey Street, maybe half a mile away from the ocean. It was a two-story colonial house faced with brick. The shutters were dark green. The front door was white. Ivy had grown halfway up the front of the house.

Mrs. Bishop answered the doorbell.

The Swampscott cop said, 'I'm Officer Antonelli, ma'am. Swampscott Police. This is Chief Jesse Stone from Paradise.'

'Is there anything wrong?' Mrs. Bishop said.

'Just a routine investigation, ma'am. May we come in?'

'Oh, certainly.'

Maybe forty-two, a lot of blond hair, a lot of eye makeup. She might have been a cheerleader. *Hell*, Jesse thought, *she might be a cheerleader*. She was wearing jeans and a white tee shirt that hung down to her thighs. In blue letters across the front was printed PERSONAL BEST.

'Hank,' she said into the kitchen, 'there are some policemen here.'

Hank appeared drinking coffee from a large mug that had the word MUG printed on it.

Everything's labeled, Jesse thought.

'Hank Bishop,' he said. 'What seems to be the problem?'

'Just routine,' Antonelli said. 'Could you tell us where your daughter is?'

'Carla's here,' Bishop said.

A girl, maybe thirteen, was standing in the doorway to the kitchen. Jesse smiled and nodded at her. She had no reaction. Antonelli looked at Jesse.

'How about Billie?' Jesse said.

'I have no daughter named Billie,' Bishop said.

'Elinor Bishop?'

'No.'

Jesse looked at the cheerleader wife. 'Mrs. Bishop?'

She shook her blond head firmly.

'No,' she said. 'We have no Elinor Bishop.'

'Do you have any other children?'

'Yes,' Bishop said. 'Carla's older sister, Emily.'

'And where is she?'

'Mount Holyoke College,' Mrs. Bishop said quickly.

'In the summer?' Jesse said.

'Many students go to college in the summer,' Mrs. Bishop said. 'Emily plans to graduate in three years.'

Jesse was watching Carla. She was motionless in the doorway. Neither in the room, nor out of it. Her face was blank.

'We have a young woman dead in Paradise,' Jesse said. 'We have reason to believe her name is Elinor Bishop, and we were led to believe that she was your daughter.'

'You were misled,' Bishop said.

'You have no daughter named Elinor Bishop?'

'We do not,' Bishop said.

Jesse looked at Mrs. Bishop. She shook her head firmly. He looked at Carla in the doorway. She seemed stiff with immobility. Her face perfectly inanimate. Jesse nodded. With his head he gestured Antonelli to the door.

'Thank you very much for your time,' he said.

14

It was Wednesday afternoon. Wednesday nights he always spent with Jenn. Jesse looked at his watch: 4:20. He took a deep breath.

'Okay,' he said. 'Let's see if we can make this thing work out.'

Molly was in the room, as she always was when they'd arrested a woman. She leaned against the wall beside Suitcase Simpson. Seated in front of Jesse in two straight-backed chairs were an unattractive man and woman who smelled strongly of alcohol. The woman had an evolving bruise on her cheekbone under her left eye. Her lower lip was fattening.

'There's nothing to work out,' the man said.

He was a middle-sized man with a beard and curly black hair. It made what showed of his face look very pale. His aviator glasses were gold-framed and tinted amber.

'It's four-twenty in the afternoon and you're both drunk,' Jesse said.

'You never had a few drinks?'

'And you were rowdy enough to cause the bartender at The Sevens to call us.'

'We had a fucking argument,' the man said. 'You never had a fucking argument with somebody?'

'And when Officer Simpson arrived you were punching out your wife in the parking lot.'

'I wasn't punching her out,' the man said.

'How many times did he hit you, ma'am?' Jesse said to the woman.

The woman shook her head.

'There's some evidence on your face for at least twice,' Jesse said.

'He didn't hit me,' she said.

Jesse glanced up at Simpson.

'I saw him hit her twice with his right fist,' Simpson said.

Molly said, 'When Suit called it in I checked the computer. This is the third time they've been in here.'

'Same occasion?' Jesse said.

'Yes.'

'And we let it go why?'

'Mrs. Snyder wouldn't file a complaint,' Molly said.

'How about this time?' Jesse said to Mrs. Snyder.

'He didn't hit me,' she said.

'Sure he did,' Jesse said. 'Didn't you, Mr. Snyder?'

Snyder shook his head. 'I didn't hit her.'

Jesse put his left elbow on the arm of his swivel chair and

rested his chin in the palm of his left hand. He looked at the Snyders for a while without speaking, then he spoke to Molly.

'There's three times we know about,' Jesse said. 'How many times you suppose it happened and we don't know about it?'

'It's usually a lot more than is reported,' Molly said.

'You got no right talking about us like that,' Snyder said. 'We didn't do anything but have a few drinks and get in a little squabble.'

The word came out 'schkwabble.' *I know the feeling*, Jesse thought.

'Molly,' Jesse said. 'I think you better take Mrs. Snyder down to Channing Hospital Emergency Room and get her face cleaned up.'

'It's okay,' Mrs. Snyder said. 'It'll be fine.'

'And while she's there have them examine her whole body.'

'Hey,' Snyder said. 'What are you gonna do, strip her down?'

'Suit, put Mr. Snyder in a cell, for his own protection, until he's sober.'

'I ain't drunk. I ain't going in no drunk tank. No way I'm letting you take her down to the fucking hospital and make her strip.'

'I don't want to go to the hospital.'

Jesse got up from behind his desk and walked around and stood in front of them and leaned his hips on the front edge of the desk.

'What's your first name, Mr. Snyder.'

'Jerry.'

'Jerry, we got you for assault.'

'I didn't assault nobody.'

'We have the bruised victim. We have the eyewitness testimony of a police officer, and I'll bet we could find some bruising on your knuckles.'

Snyder looked quickly at his hands and caught himself and looked quickly away.

'We got plenty of grounds for putting you in jail.'

'Not for doing nothing you don't.'

'But we're trying not to turn this into something bigger than it is,' Jesse said. 'So you'll have to sit it out here for a couple hours while we get some medical opinion on the extent of the damage.'

'You can't arrest me, I don't got a lawyer.'

'We're not arresting you, Jerry. We're detaining you in the interests of public safety, and your own. You're too drunk to be out loose.'

'I won't go in no jail cell,' Snyder said.

He stood up, his face less than a foot from Jesse's.

'Come on, Viv,' he said to his wife. 'We're walking.'

Jesse shook his head slightly and kicked Snyder's ankles out from under him. Snyder went down suddenly, on his left side. Before Snyder could reorient himself, Simpson stepped from the wall, snapped the cuffs on him, and got him on his feet.

'Jerry,' Mrs. Snyder said.

'You'll see him in a couple of hours,' Jesse said. 'Nobody's going to hurt him.'

'He didn't do nothing,' she said as Molly steered her out of the room.

15

They went to the Gray Gull every Wednesday night. They sat outside in the warm night where they could look at the town dock and the harbor and across the harbor at Paradise Neck and Stiles Island. Jenn had a glass of Chardonnay. Jesse drank cranberry juice and soda.

'Are you solving your murder?' Jenn asked.

'Not exactly,' Jesse said.

'Progress?'

'Some.'

'Try not to be such a blabbermouth,' Jenn said.

Jesse smiled. 'I'm preoccupied with you,' he said.

'I'm not sure that's good for you. But I guess I like it.'

'I thought I had the dead girl ID'd,' Jesse said. 'But the people who were supposed to be her parents say they have no such daughter.'

'Well, they would know, wouldn't they?'

'One of the daughters they do have was there,' Jesse said. 'Younger. Maybe twelve, thirteen.'

'So?'

'There was something wrong. Kid looked like she'd been frozen.'

'Wrong?'

'Yep.'

'You think parents would pretend not to have a child? When they really did?'

'Maybe.'

'Why?'

'Maybe she was bad. Maybe it was one of those never darken my door again. I no longer have a daughter things.'

'So you can find that out, can't you?'

'I can. I haven't yet.'

'They have any other children?'

'Yes. An older daughter. She's at Mount Holyoke College. We called and left a message. She hasn't called back.'

'How can a parent deny a child?' Jenn said.

'I've seen it before,' Jesse said. 'Kid disappoints the parent. Parent can't stand the disappointment. If the kid doesn't exist, then the disappointment doesn't exist.'

He sipped some cranberry juice and soda.

'It's hard to live with the fact of your own failure every day,' he said.

'I know.'

'We both live with that,' Jesse said.

'It's my fault,' Jenn said. 'I'm the adulteress.'

'And I'm the drunk,' Jesse said. 'It does no good, Jenn.'

'I know.'

The black water moved quietly against the pilings beneath the deck. The light gleamed singularly at the end of Paradise

Neck. Some of the big pleasure boats in the harbor were lighted. People sat, mostly on the afterdeck, and drank cocktails.

They looked at their menus. They both ordered lobster salad.

'You know what my shrink told me?' Jenn said.

Jesse smiled. 'No,' he said. 'I don't.'

'He said that the bond between us was truly impressive.'

'Even though we're divorced,' Jesse said.

'Maybe more so because we're not together.'

'So the bond has to be strong,' Jesse said.

'It's all there is to hold us,' Jenn said.

'Maybe it shouldn't,' Jesse said. 'Maybe we should move on.'

'We should,' Jenn said.

'But we don't,' Jesse said.

'We can't,' Jenn said.

'But we don't get married.'

'I can't,' Jenn said.

'And we're not monogamous.'

'When I think of it,' Jenn said. 'You and me, till death do us part ... I feel claustrophobic.'

'You and the shrink figured out why that is?'

'Not yet,' Jenn said.

Jesse looked at Jenn's face. He knew it so well. He felt the need begin to rise like water filling a glass. He wanted a drink. Something more than cranberry juice. He felt that need rising too, and the needs became one need. He took in some air. *Hang on.* He took in a big breath and exhaled slowly, trying not to let it show. Jenn put her hand out and rested it on his hand.

'But we will,' she said.

'I hope so,' Jesse said.

His voice was flat with the effort of repression.

'I do too,' Jenn said.

'Maybe you and he will find a way to break the bond,' Jesse said.

'I don't think so,' Jenn said.

'Good.'

'This is very hard,' Jenn said.

'It is.'

Jenn's hand was still resting on his forearm.

'But we're still here,' Jenn said softly.

'We are,' Jesse said.

16

'What makes you think she'll show up here?' Molly said.

She sat beside Jesse in his unmarked car, parked across from an ice cream stand on the Lynn Shore Drive, above the beach.

'Lilly Summers told me the kids hang out here.'

'The principal?'

'Un-huh.'

'Did she also tell you that school records show Billie Bishop's parents to be Henry and Sandra Bishop?'

'Actually,' Jesse grinned at Molly, 'she told you that when you called her.'

'Nice to be remembered,' Molly said. 'So why don't you just confront them with the record?'

'I thought I might learn more by talking to the kid first,' Jesse said, 'before everybody shuts down because they're scared or mad or defensive or whatever they'll get.'

'You only saw her that one time,' Molly said. 'You sure you'll recognize her?'

Jesse smiled.

'Of course you will,' Molly said. 'Cancel the question.'

It was a still July day. There was no air movement. The foliage in the little park looked thick and permanent. The ocean was still. Insects hummed. Around the ice cream stand young kids gathered in a colorful confusion of tee shirts, shorts, high-priced sneakers, and expensive bicycles. Occasionally someone bought ice cream.

'They're the right age group,' Jesse said.

'Twelve to fourteen,' Molly said. 'I got a couple.'

'Tough being that age,' Jesse said.

'Tough being a kid,' Molly said.

Jesse nodded. He looked steadily across the street at the kids.

'This principal,' Molly said, 'Dr. Summers?'

Jesse nodded.

'How's she look?'

'Good,' Jesse said.

Molly waited. Jesse kept looking at the kids.

'Anything there?' Molly said.

'You mean sex?' Jesse said.

'Sure,' Molly said. 'Or romance, or companionship, or fun.'

'Not while you're still around,' Jesse said.

Molly laughed.

'I'm a married Irish Catholic,' she said. 'I don't do any of that stuff.'

'So how come you got four kids?'

'I have to sleep sometime,' Molly said. 'What about Doc Summers?'

Jesse smiled.

'If she presses me,' Jesse said, 'I may have to sleep with her.'

Carla Bishop pedaled up on a black mountain bike with green striping.

'There's the sister,' Jesse said.

Carla was talking with some animation to three other girls near the corner of the ice cream stand. The two cops got out of the car and moved across through the crowd. Molly was in uniform. Jesse was not. Those kids that noticed at all eyed the two adults with a mixture of suspicion and contempt. Jesse stopped in front of Carla and waited until she finished a sentence.

Then he took his badge out and showed it to her and said, 'Hello, Carla, remember me?'

She turned and stared at him. She looked at Molly in uniform beside him.

'Jesse Stone,' he said. 'I was at your home the other day.'

'What do you want?' she said.

'This is Molly Crane,' Jesse said.

'She your wife?'

'She's a cop,' Jesse said. 'Like me. We need to talk with you, and are willing to bribe you with the ice cream of your choice.'

'Big fucking deal,' Carla said.

'Okay, no ice cream. We still need to talk.'

'About what?'

The other kids had gathered into an audience and Carla was playing to them.

'About Billie.'

'Billie?'

'Your sister,' Jesse said.

'My sister's name is Emily and she's at college.'

'Your other sister. Billie. The one your parents won't talk about.'

Carla was silent.

Someone in the audience said, 'Billie the Bopper.'

Some of the kids snickered.

'Shut up,' Carla said.

'Why don't we go sit in the car,' Molly said, 'and we can talk.'

'How come you're a cop?' Carla said to Molly.

It was a sullen question. But even as she asked it, she started to move toward the car. Molly smiled at her as they walked across the street.

'I got sick of being a movie star,' Molly said.

17

Molly was in the backseat. Carla sat in the front seat with Jesse.

'Do I have to talk with you?' Carla asked Jesse.

'Not yet.'

'Shouldn't I have a lawyer or something?'

'You're not under arrest,' Jesse said. 'We just need to know about your sister Billie.'

'You think she's dead?'

'Yes.'

'Can't you tell if it's her by looking?'

'No.'

Carla was silent.

'So why do you think it's her?'

'The young woman we found was wearing Hooker Royce's class ring on a chain around her neck,' Jesse said.

'Does Hooker know where she is?'

'I talked with him on the phone,' Molly said. 'He doesn't.'

Carla's face was pinched, and there was a tightness around her mouth. But Jesse saw no sign of tears.

'What happened to her?' Carla said.

'Someone shot her,' Jesse said, 'and put her body in a lake.'

'Jesus,' Carla said.

'Yes.'

All three of them were quiet, listening to the air-conditioning in the unmarked police car.

'Do my parents know?' Carla said.

'Only what you heard me tell them,' Jesse said.

Again the soft sound of the air-conditioning. Across the street the kids were back to hanging out, but most of them looked regularly over at the car.

'Who did it?' Carla said.

'Don't know,' Jesse said. 'We're still trying to identify the body.'

'You're just a bunch of hick cops anyway,' Carla said. 'You'll never find out.'

'Do you have a family dentist?' Jesse said.

'Of course.'

'What's his name?'

'Dr. Levine. Why?'

'It might help us identify the victim,' Jesse said.

'Can't you just use fingerprints?' Carla said.

'Do you know where Billie is?' Jesse said.

'No.'

'When's the last time you saw her?'

Carla shrugged.

'When's the last time she was home?'

'They kicked her out right after school ended.'

'Your mother and father kicked her out?'

'Yes.'

'Because?'

'They said she was a druggie and a whore.'

'Was she?'

Carla shrugged again.

'Did they tell you not to talk about it?'

Carla didn't answer. She was motionless, looking at her knees.

'What did they say, Carla?' Molly asked.

Carla answered without raising her eyes.

'They said there was only two of us now. Me and Emily.'

Her voice was very small.

'Have you heard from her since she left?' Jesse said.

'No.'

'How do you feel about all this?' Molly said.

Carla shrugged again, concentrating on her knees. 'Billie messed up,' she said.

'Are you scared you might mess up?' Molly said.

Carla didn't say anything. Molly took a card case from her shirt pocket, selected a card, and handed it to Carla.

'If you do mess up,' Molly said, 'you can call me. I'll help you.'

Carla still didn't speak. But she took the card.

18

Lilly lived in a condominium apartment on the fifth floor in a vast sprawl of condominium apartments just off Route 1A behind a shopping mall near the Salem line. It was five minutes past seven when Jesse arrived at her door carrying a bottle of Iron Horse champagne. She was wearing faded blue jeans, carefully pressed, a white silk blouse with a stand-up collar, and short black boots with thick heels. The jeans were snug. The blouse was open at the neck and a gold chain showed against her light tan.

'Do you have a warrant?' Lilly said.

'No,' Jesse said. 'But I've got a bottle of champagne.'

Lilly smiled.

'That will do,' she said. 'Come on in.'

The apartment had white walls and blond furniture and sand-colored carpeting. There were sliders at the end of the living room that opened onto a small balcony that allowed you to look down at the back side of the shopping mall. The furniture was appropriate without being interesting.

'Don't judge me by my home,' Lilly said. 'I bought it after my second divorce, furniture and all, and moved in until I found something a little better.'

'And?'

'And I haven't gotten around to looking.'

'Too busy?' Jesse said.

'Do I have the right to an attorney?' Lilly said.

'Sorry. Sometimes I think I've asked too many questions for too long a time.'

Lilly held out the champagne bottle.

'Shall we begin by drinking this?' she said.

Jesse hesitated. Club soda would be the right thing to drink. He took the bottle.

'We'd be fools not to,' he said.

She got an ice bucket and glasses and set them on the glass-top coffee table. Jesse uncorked the wine and poured some in each glass. They clinked glasses and held each other's look for a moment and drank.

'I love champagne,' Lilly said.

Jesse nodded.

'Actually,' Lilly said, 'I love having someone to drink it with.'

'Lucky I stopped by,' Jesse said.

'It wasn't luck. I invited you for dinner.'

'That's right.'

They drank. *Sip*, Jesse told himself. *Sip*.

'I guess, if I had to be completely honest …' Lilly said.

'No need for that,' Jesse said.

'I guess I'm still here for sort of the same reason. I guess I was hoping for someone to come along who would look for a new place with me.'

'Would that include either ex-husband?'

'No,' Lilly said. 'It would not.'

They were quiet, both thinking of other lives they had lived, other nights in twosomes with champagne. He could feel the charge between them. Simultaneous release and tension. Since he'd first been in her office he'd known it would come to this, and now it had. He felt the relaxation of arrival. Soon he'd see her naked. Soon there would be no tension.

'Animosity?' Jesse said.

'With my exes? Not the first one. He's nice. He lives in Chicago now, works as a construction supervisor for a big company. I see him occasionally when he comes to Boston.'

'So what happened?'

'I don't know, exactly. You go along thinking it's forever, then one day it isn't. One day he didn't want to be married to me, and I didn't want to be married to him.'

'Somebody else?'

'No. It was more that we hoped for someone else. Or something else. Our marriage just wasn't enough.'

'How about number two?' Jesse said.

'The sonovabitch,' Lilly said, and pretended to spit.

'Another woman?'

'Another dozen,' Lilly said.

'Animosity,' Jesse said.

'A lot,' Lilly said.

'How long have you been single?' Jesse said.

'Five years.'

'You mind living alone?'

'Yes.'

They were quiet again.

'You?' Lilly said.

'No,' Jesse said. 'I don't mind living alone.... I mind being alone. And I mind Jenn not being alone.'

'You're pretty hooked into Jenn,' Lilly said.

'I am.'

'How long have you been divorced?'

'Four years.'

'I'm not sure that's very good for you,' Lilly said.

'Probably not,' Jesse said.

'Have you ever seen a shrink?'

'No.'

'Maybe you should. It helps.'

'Maybe I should,' Jesse said.

'But?'

'My father was a cop,' Jesse said. 'My whole life I been playing ball, or I been a cop.'

'So?'

'Seeing a psychiatrist is not something cops and ballplayers are supposed to do.'

'What are they supposed to do?'

Jesse paused, thinking about it.

'They're supposed to hang in.'

'Forever?'

'As needed,' Jesse said.

Lilly looked at him thoughtfully. 'Wow,' she said. 'You need a shrink worse than I thought.'

'Jenn says so, too.'

'She seeing one?'

'Yes.'

'Well,' Lilly said. 'You'll go when you're ready.'

Jesse didn't say anything. Maybe he would. But if he did, it would start with the provision that he wasn't going to stop loving Jenn. The champagne was gone so quickly. *You have to concentrate every minute*, Jesse thought.

'I have made us a lovely supper,' Lilly said.

'I could use one,' Jesse said.

'But if we eat it first,' Lilly said, 'we'll both be thinking about afterwards and how that's going to go, and won't be able to enjoy the dinner as we should.'

'That is a problem,' Jesse said.

'So I think we should have the afterwards first. Then we'd be free to concentrate on the lovely supper.'

'Sure,' Jesse said.

Lilly put down her champagne glass and stood.

'Follow me,' she said, and walked past the kitchen counter toward her bedroom.

He felt the familiar smooth curve as he ran his hand up her thigh. The familiar soft slope of her belly. He had done this often. This time, like each time, it was brand-new. He could hear her breathing, felt the pressure of her hips, she was skillful and fully engaged. The part of him that was not making love smiled. Didn't matter if she was skillful. His father used to say, the worst piece of ass I ever had was excellent. There was always that part. The one that wasn't engaged, whether it was lovemaking or fighting. There was always the amused, non-judgmental *other* observing it. He wondered if she had an *other*.

Finally, dressed and relaxed, they sat at her glass-top dining table and ate in silence in the gently moving light of the candles Lilly had lighted. There was a bottle of white wine at hand in an ice bucket.

'That's your real hair color,' he said.

'My hair turned silver when I was twenty-six,' Lilly said.

She poured some white wine into Jesse's glass. *It's all right. I'm nowhere near drunk.* He drank some. *Nice wine.* He ate some of the supper she had served them.

'What am I eating?' Jesse said.

'Lobster meat in a light cream sauce,' Lilly said. 'With sherry, pearl onions and mushrooms and different-colored sweet peppers, over basmati rice.'

'You can cook.'

Lilly smiled at him.

'Second best thing I do,' she said.

Jesse nodded several times and drank some wine.

19

Jesse was pretty sure that things would go better with Hooker Royce if his parents weren't around when they talked. He found Hooker at the high school, on the football field, running sprints. He had on expensive athletic shoes, a stopwatch on his wrist and a pair of gray cotton sweatpants that had been cut off to mid thigh. Jesse stood quietly watching Hooker as he did forty-yard sprints, timing each one. He was a muscular, in-shape, middle-sized kid, a little bigger than Jesse, with an even tan and a blond crew cut. When Hooker paused to rest, Jesse spoke to him.

'My name's Jesse Stone. I'm with the police in Paradise.'

'Is it about Billie?'

'It is.'

'I don't know where she is. I already told the lady from your department that called me.'

Jesse nodded. They began to walk around the quarter-mile track that circled the field.

'When's football start at Yale?' Jesse said.

'I'm supposed to show up day after Labor Day.'

'You a running back?' Jesse said.

'Yes.'

'What'd you run out of in high school?' Jesse said.

'Deep back in the I. You play?'

'High school,' Jesse said. 'You plan to show up in shape.'

'Be dumb not to,' Hooker said.

'You were a *Globe* all-scholastic in three sports,' Jesse said.

Hooker nodded.

'And an honor student.'

Hooker nodded again.

'Full boat to Yale?'

'Yes.'

'You're a nice-looking kid,' Jesse said.

'Thank you.'

'Probably don't have much trouble getting a date,' Jesse said.

Hooker grinned. 'When I have time,' he said.

'So how come Billie?' Jesse said.

'Whaddya mean?'

'Billie doesn't seem like she'd be your girlfriend.'

'Girlfriend? She wasn't my girlfriend.'

'You gave her your class ring,' Jesse said.

'Yeah, but that was …'

They stopped walking. Hooker turned toward Jesse.

'It's like, I broke up with my regular girlfriend.'

'And Billie was available?'

'Christ,' Hooker said, and smiled. 'Billie was always available.'

'And?'

'And, yeah, I needed a date for senior prom, and Paula was going with somebody else.'

'And the pickings were thin.'

'Most of the girls already had dates. And it seemed like a way to stick it to Paula.'

'And get laid in the process,' Jesse said.

Hooker grinned and shrugged.

'So how come the ring?' Jesse said.

'I kind of liked her,' Hooker said. 'After I actually took her to the dance. And I felt bad for her. I mean everybody was banging her, but nobody cared anything much about her, you know?'

'Un-huh.'

'And, you know, she wasn't that bad a kid. Like everybody thought she was stupid, and she wasn't. She was pretty smart about a lot of stuff.'

'And you fell head over heels in love,' Jesse said.

'What planet you come from?' Hooker said. 'Like I said, I felt bad for her. I'm not going out with anybody. So I figure, hell, I'm going to college in a couple of months. I'll give her the ring, make her feel good, and then I'll go to college in September and it's over. I don't give a shit about the ring.'

'She know that?' Jesse said.

'No, of course not. But it didn't work out like I thought. Paula and I patched it up, and she said if we were going to be together I couldn't be going out with Billie.'

'Seems fair,' Jesse said. 'To Paula.'

'Yeah, and, like, I love Paula. You know? Billie wasn't so bad. But …'

'When'd you break the news?' Jesse said.

'About a week after graduation,' Hooker said.

'How'd she take it?'

'Funny,' Hooker said. 'She was funny about it like she expected it to happen. I told her to keep the ring. Like a memento. I figured I'd give Paula something from Yale.'

They were quiet, sitting together on the bottom row of the empty stands with the summer sun staring down at them.

'What was her life like at home?' Jesse said.

'I don't know,' Hooker said. 'She never said anything about home.'

'And you never went there?'

'Couple times to pick her up. Mrs. Bishop's real young-looking.'

'Anything else?'

Hooker shrugged.

'Nothing I can think of. I'd just go in, pick up Billie, and we'd leave. Mrs. Bishop seemed nice. I was surprised when they kicked her out.'

'Did you see her after they kicked her out?'

'No.'

'You know where she went?'

'No.'

They were silent again. Jesse liked to leave openings for people to fill.

'I gotta do my sprints,' Hooker said.

'Sure,' Jesse said. 'You know anyone with a reason to kill her?'

'No,' Hooker said. 'You think it's her?'

'Probably,' Jesse said.

'Jesus,' Hooker said. 'That's a shame.'

'It is,' Jesse said.

'You think you can catch him?'

'Or her.'

'Him or her,' Hooker said. 'You think you'll catch him?'

'You think you'll make the Yale football team?' Jesse said.

'Sure. You gotta stay positive. If you think you can't, you probably won't.'

Jesse smiled and didn't say anything.

Hooker saw the smile and paused.

'Oh,' he said. 'Yeah, sure. Well, good luck.'

'You, too,' Jesse said.

Hooker walked back to the field, stood on the forty-yard line, set his stopwatch and sprinted to the end zone.

He probably will make it.

20

No one groomed the field they played on. The park department mowed it once a week, but that was all. Sometimes somebody on one of the teams would bring down a rake and try to smooth things out a little, but there were too many games, and everyone had jobs, and there was just time to come home and change and get to the park. There wasn't much time for groundskeeping. The right-hand batter's box had holes worn in it by an endless series of right-handed hitters digging in. Whatever your natural batting stance, you were forced to set your feet in the holes.

Jesse didn't like it. When he'd played he'd hit with a slightly open stance. The holes in the batter's box forced him to close it up. On the other hand the ball was fat, and it came a lot slower than it had in the minor leagues. And why did he care anyway? Jesse smiled to himself. Pride. The fact of having been good carried with it its own responsibility. He was supposed to be the best player in the league. It mattered.

The pitcher wasn't good. Some of the guys in the league could bring it, and the pitcher's mound was much closer in softball. But this guy couldn't throw hard. He was getting by with slow and slower, trying to move the ball around. Each at bat, the pitcher had worked Jesse high and low. He worked everyone high and low. The first pitch was high. The second pitch was low. With a one-one count, Jesse shifted his hands slightly so he could uppercut the ball. When the pitch arrived, shoulder high, he hit it over the left-fielder's head. There were no fences. You had to run out the home runs. Jesse could still run. Between short and third he saw the left fielder give up on the ball. Jesse slowed to a jog as he rounded third. He got an assortment of low and high fives when he crossed home plate. Just as if it mattered.

21

He met Emily Bishop in a coffee shop in a small shopping center near the town common. She wore the gray tee shirt she had promised to wear. It was too big for her. PROPERTY OF SWAMPSCOTT ATHLETIC DEPARTMENT was printed across the front. Below the tee shirt were baggy blue jeans held up by wide blue suspenders. Her feet were up on the chair next to her. She was wearing lace-up black boots with thick soles. Her hair was very short. Her face was without makeup. The hint of a good figure showed through the jeans and tee shirt. A pack of Marlboros lay on the table in front of her. She was smoking and drinking coffee. He wondered if Billie looked like her.

Jesse stopped at the counter and got a large coffee with cream and sugar and brought it over to the table where Emily was sitting. She'd already decided who he was.

'I'm Jesse Stone,' he said.

'Show me your badge,' Emily said.

She had a flat, unpleasant voice. Jesse showed her his badge.

'Christ,' she said. 'The fucking chief.'

'It's nothing,' Jesse said.

'So what happened to my sister?' Emily said.

There was no way to soften it. Jesse had long since learned to just say it.

'We think she was shot in the head and dumped in a lake in Paradise.'

'You think?'

'Body is hard to identify.'

'So why do you think it's my sister?'

Jesse told her. Emily smoked her cigarette and drank some coffee and listened with no expression.

'Billie, Billie,' she said when Jesse finished.

Jesse took a sip of his coffee. He waited. Emily dropped her cigarette into the half inch of coffee in the bottom of her cup.

'Christ, didn't they fuck her up,' Emily said.

'Parents?'

'Of course, parents. Probably fucked me up, too. Except I got out in time, maybe.'

How and why they had fucked up their daughters was interesting, but it didn't lead Jesse anywhere he wanted to go at the moment.

'Do you have a picture of your sister?' Jesse said.

'Not her alone,' Emily said. 'But I got a picture in the dorm of her and me and Carla.'

'I'd like to borrow it,' Jesse said. 'I promise I'll get it back to you.'

Emily nodded.

'When they kicked Billie out,' Jesse said, 'do you know where she went?'

'Someplace in Boston.'

'You know where?'

'No. Some nun runs it.'

'A shelter?'

'I guess.'

'She get along okay with Hooker?' Jesse said.

'Hooker was nice to her,' Emily said.

'Anybody that might have harmed her?'

'Half the guys in the high school were bopping her. Probably some older guys, too.'

'Any names?'

'No. I don't know. She thought it made her popular. I didn't want to hear about it.'

'Anything else you can tell me that might help?'

Emily lit another cigarette and inhaled deeply and let it out slowly though her nose. There was something practiced about it, Jesse thought, as if it were a trick recently learned.

'I got a letter from her back in my room,' she said. 'I think she said the nun's name in it.'

'Can we get that? When I pick up the picture?'

'Yeah, sure.'

They were silent. Jesse watched her smoke. He could see her eyes well up, but she didn't cry.

'You okay?' he said.

'Yeah, sure.'

'Can we get the picture and the letter?'

'Yeah, sure.'

They left the coffee shop and walked to the campus. Jesse thought how different it would feel to go there and graduate. Old stone, old trees, wide paths, white houses with dark shutters, green grass in spring, new snow glistening in winter. Different from being a desert high school grad with a sore arm.

In Emily's room there were clothes on the floor in a pile. The bed was unmade. On her desk, books and papers were jumbled with no pattern. Amidst the jumble was a framed picture of the Bishop girls. In color, all smiling at the camera.

'How old is the picture?' Jesse said.

'Last summer.'

Jesse stared at it while Emily looked in her desk drawer and in a moment came out with a letter. It was postmarked July 3. Emily handed it to him and Jesse took it. She picked up the picture and handed it to Jesse.

'The happy family,' Emily said.

Jesse took the picture.

'I hope Carla gets out before they get her, too.'

Jesse didn't comment. There wasn't any comment to make.

'They aren't going to get me,' Emily said. 'I'm outta there. I'm on my own and I'm never going back.'

'Your father still pay your tuition?'

'Of course he does. You think he wants to have his daughter drop out of a seven fucking sisters school?'

'Good to be able to count on something,' Jesse said.

'Fuck him,' Emily said. 'He owes it to me. I'll take him for everything he's got if I can.'

Quite suddenly she began to cry. Jesse put an arm on her shoulder. She shrugged it off and stepped away from him. He stood quietly in the room without touching her until she stopped crying.

'You got someone to talk to?' Jesse said.

She nodded.

'Shrink?'

She nodded again. Jesse took out a card.

'You think of anything … or you need anything.'

He handed her the card. She looked at it as if it meant more than it did.

'You'll do that?' Jesse said.

'Yes.'

'Might be good if you called your shrink,' Jesse said.

She didn't speak or move. Jesse stood for another moment and then he left.

22

Jesse stood in the open slider of his condo, looking out over his balcony toward Paradise Neck. Below the balcony the black water of the harbor moved with aimless purpose against the rust-colored rocks. Jesse liked the sound. He would like it even more with a drink. He knew the girl was Billie Bishop. He couldn't exactly prove it yet, but he knew. He knew there was something wrong in the Bishop house. Were the girls being molested? They seemed angry. Especially Emily. He thought about how pleasant it would be to sit on his balcony with a tall scotch and soda and look at the harbor and listen to the gentle sway of the Atlantic Ocean and not think about molestation. He wondered if Emily was a lesbian. As the evening lengthened it grew dark enough for the lights of the big houses on the neck to show across the harbor. He wished Jenn were here. He wished they could sit together and look at the ocean and the far lights.

He got up and walked into his kitchen. He took a glass down from the cupboard, sixteen ounces, the kind you got when you ordered a pint of Guinness. He filled the glass with ice cubes, poured two inches of Dewar's into the glass, and opened a can of club soda and filled the rest of the glass with it. He took a spoon from the drawer and stirred the glass until the colorless soda diluted the amber scotch evenly. He took a sip. Perfect. He brought the glass out onto the balcony and sat down with his feet on the railing. He drank another sip. There was no hurry to get it in. There was a half gallon in there on the kitchen counter. There were twelve cans of soda in the cupboard. The ice maker in the refrigerator was perpetual. He was only going to have a couple. But it was comforting to know that there was enough.

There was enough moonlight for Jesse to see the boats waiting at their moorings. Toward the outer harbor a single boat with bow lights cut across the harbor toward the town wharf. Jesse had another sip. Probably the harbor master. It was Friday night. He wasn't scheduled to see Jenn until Wednesday. From the deck Jesse could smell the hint of clams frying at the Gray Gull, two blocks away. The smell was comforting. He thought about Billie Bishop's picture. It was better to think of her in the picture. In the picture she was smiling. Probably doing what she was told to do. Cops see kids like Billie too often. Town pump. Kids so desperate for affection or connection or whatever it was that sex became their handshake. They were joyless encounters as far as he knew. For certain, it was not pleasure that drove girls like Billie to flop for anybody.

His drink was gone. One more. He got up and went to the kitchen and made another one and brought it back to the deck. The scotch made him feel integrated, complete. *Not a wild drunk*, Jesse thought. *Mostly quiet.* Mostly the booze enriched him. Jenn wasn't nasty about his drinking. She had too much psychotherapy not to understand the struggle. But she didn't know the feeling that when you were feeling it made it one you wouldn't want to miss. Why would somebody shoot a kid like Billie? She could have been simply wrong place/wrong time. But that theory led him nowhere. Better to think about promiscuity. He took a swallow of scotch and soda. Sex was the only thing he knew about her that could have gotten her killed.

From the parking lot, out of sight of his balcony, Jesse heard a car door slam and the sound of brisk high heels. The front hall door of Jesse's building opened and closed. Jesse took another swallow. Sometimes on Wednesdays when Jenn came, they would have sex. Often they would not. It depended mostly, he guessed, on what was going on in her therapy. He also was pretty sure that if she were having sex with someone else, she wouldn't have sex with him, and vice versa. It was an odd standard, Jesse thought. But it was a standard. He had no such standard. He would sleep with Lilly Summers on a Tuesday and Jenn on a Wednesday and be pleased about both.

Though he knew that if his relationship with Jenn hinged on it, he would develop such a standard on the spot. He smiled a little that he was having sex with a school principal. He drank some scotch. He wondered about Marcy Campbell. Maybe it was time to have sex with her again, also. Jesse Stone at stud. And he was going to find the sonovabitch who killed that kid, too. His drink was gone. He looked at the glass for a long moment. He didn't want to give up the sense of wholeness. He took in some air and let it out slowly.

Out loud he said, 'Fuck it,' his voice intrusive in the pale darkness. Then he stood and went to the kitchen and made another drink.

23

It took Molly a day on the phone to find the shelters in Boston run by nuns. There were three. Jesse found the right nun on his first try. Her name was Sister Mary John and she ran a shelter in the basement of a church in Jamaica Plain. When Jesse came in, Sister was sitting on the corner of a plywood banquet table with folding metal legs that obviously served as her desk. She was red-haired, wearing a black sweat suit with a white stripe on the sleeves. The only sign of her calling was a small gold cross on a thin gold chain that hung around her neck.

'Are you sure you're a nun?' Jesse said.

'Pretty sure,' Sister said.

Jesse smiled.

'You talked with Molly Crane on the phone about a missing girl.'

'Yes.'

Jesse took out a blowup of Billie, processed from the family picture, and held it out for Sister Mary John to look at. Sister nodded her head slowly.

'When was she here?' Jesse said.

'Beginning of the summer,' Sister said.

'She's not here now?'

'No.'

'Would you tell me if she were?' Jesse said.

'It would depend on who you were and why you wanted to know.'

'You know who I am,' Jesse said. 'We think Billie was murdered.'

Sister's face softened for a moment.

'Think?'

'Know, but can't prove. Condition of the body makes it hard.'

Sister nodded.

A young black woman with a ring through one nostril came into the room and saw Jesse and, without changing her pace, turned and left.

'Am I that obvious?' Jesse said.

'A cop is a cop is a cop,' Sister said. 'My girls have learned to be alert.'

'Do you know where Billie went when she left here?'

'I have a phone number. We'd agreed I would only give it to her older sister or somebody named Hooker.'

'Did you give it to either?'

'Neither of them asked.'

'May I have the phone number?' Jesse said.

Sister looked at him for a time.

'She's dead,' Jesse said. 'I'm trying to find who killed her.'

Sister nodded. She reached under the desk and pulled a yellow plastic milk crate toward her. It was full of file folders. She riffled through them, pulled one out, and took from it a single sheet of paper. She looked at the sheet and copied the number onto a little pad of stickum notes.

'Ever call the number?' Jesse said.

'No.'

'When the girls are at the shelter they don't stay here, do they?'

'No. We are what the name implies, a shelter. They come, they go. They know they have a place to sleep if they need it. They know we will feed them.'

'How long was Billie here?'

Sister looked at her sheet of paper.

'Two weeks,' she said.

'Did she tell you why she was leaving?'

'She said she had a job.'

'She say where?'

'No.'

'How about the rest of the staff?' Jesse said.

Sister smiled. Jesse liked her smile.

'It's pretty much a one-nun show,' she said.

24

Jenn was doing a stand-up outside a junior high school. It was part of a station promotion campaign designed to prove once again that Channel 3 was an integral part of the community. Jesse parked on the street and walked to the shoot. He stood outside the shot while Jenn did a cute weather quiz and wrapped the segment. She saw him while she was wrapping, and as soon as it was over, she came to Jesse and kissed him lightly on the lips.

'Did you know the answers to my weather quiz?' she said.

'Do you?'

'I will when the time comes,' she said.

'Does anyone care what the answers are?' Jesse said.

'Not that I know of,' Jenn answered.

She turned to the crew.

'This is my starter husband,' she said.

The crew smiled. Jesse smiled, too.

'Kerry Roberts with the camera; Dolly Edwards, makeup; and Tracy Mayo, my producer.'

They all said hello.

'You guys pack up and take off,' Jenn told the crew. 'I'll go with Jesse.'

'How about you pack up,' Dolly said. 'And I go with Jesse.'

Everybody laughed, and Jenn put her arm through Jesse's and they walked to his car.

'What about that girl?'

'Billie?'

'You sound like she's someone you know.'

'Yeah, sometimes you get that way. You spend so much time thinking about a victim that you're surprised when you remember you've never met them.'

'So you know who she is now,' Jenn said.

'I know. I'm not sure I can prove it yet. But I know it's Billie.'

As he drove, Jesse took a manila envelope down from the car visor and took out a picture of Billie.

'It's blown up from a small picture of the family.'

'She's cute,' Jenn said.

'I guess so.'

'Smile looks awfully forced though.'

'Everybody's smile looks forced in a posed picture,' Jesse said, 'except you professionals.'

'That would be me,' Jenn said. 'A big-time professional doing weather quizzes in front of a junior high school.'

'Show biz isn't for sissies,' Jesse said.

They had dinner in Cambridge, at a new restaurant called Oleanna, which Jenn was frantic to try. The restaurant was good, but Jesse knew it meant they probably weren't going to sleep together. When Jenn was prepared to have sex she always came to Paradise and spent the night with Jesse. He rarely spent the night at her place. Someday, when the balance between them wasn't so delicate, maybe he'd ask her why. For now he knew it was an evening that would end when he drove her home.

'Have you been drinking lately?' Jenn said in the car.

'Now and then,' Jesse said.

'You didn't drink anything tonight.'

'No.'

'Why not?' Jenn said.

'Scared to, I guess,' Jesse said.

'Scared of what?'

'Scared it will get out.'

'It?'

'How I feel. I love you. I'm mad at you. I'm jealous. I'm full of, hell, I don't know, yearning, I guess. I have to keep it in its cage.'

'And you're afraid if you drink it will jump out.'

'Yeah.'

'So you drink alone?'

'Yeah.'

'So if it gets out there's no one around.'

Jesse nodded. He could feel Jenn looking at him.

'What I don't understand,' Jenn said, 'is, if you can choose not to drink sometimes, why can't you choose not to drink all the time?'

'I don't know.'

They drove over the Longfellow Bridge in silence.

When they reached the Charles Street circle, Jenn said, 'You need help with this, Jesse.'

Jesse shrugged.

'You don't have to start big,' Jenn said. 'Maybe just talk to a guy, about drinking.'

'You know a guy?' Jesse said.

'Yes.'

'How do you know a guy?'

'My shrink told me.'

'You been talking about me in therapy?' Jesse said.

Jenn laughed gently. 'Of course,' she said. 'Would you go talk to this guy? I can make you an appointment.'

'He a psychiatrist?'

'No. He's not a doctor. He's just somebody that has had some success helping people with drinking.'

'You ever meet him?'

'Yes. I went to see him.'

'About me?'

'Yes.'

It went through him viscerally, shimmering along the nerve traces. Jolting his stomach. He was part of her therapy. She was trying to help him. He was still in her life. He mattered.

'If I go,' Jesse said, 'I can make the appointment.'

25

Molly was at the front desk when Jesse came into the station carrying coffee in a paper cup.

'We found Dr. Levine,' Molly said.

'Billie's dentist.'

'Yes. Suit brought the dental chart over that we got off the body.'

'And?'

'It's her.'

Jesse nodded. There was no satisfaction in it. He sort of wished it wasn't Billie.

'You call that phone number from Sister Mary John?'

'Yes,' Molly said, and looked down at her notepad. 'Development Associates of Boston. Nobody there ever heard of Billie.'

'Or so they say.'

Molly smiled. 'Or so they say.'

'What's the address there?' Jesse said.

Molly gave it to him. 'You going to talk with them?'

'Yes.'

'Before you go we need to talk about Mr. and Mrs. Snyder,' Molly said.

'The Bickersons?'

'She's in the hospital.'

'How bad?' Jesse said.

'Nothing fatal – concussion, couple of fractures. The ER called us.'

'Her husband put her there?'

'That's what she told the ER doctor.'

'Didn't we send her down there the last time we had them in?'

'Yes. They found a lot of old injuries.'

'And?'

'She swore they were skiing injuries. Said her husband didn't hit her,' Molly said. 'DeAngelo talked with an assistant DA who said if she stuck to her story, there wasn't enough of a case.'

'I figured that,' Jesse said. 'I was hoping he might get scared.'

'Booze,' Molly said.

Jesse nodded.

'So how come she's blowing the whistle this time?'

'Maybe enough is enough,' Molly said. 'Suit's on his way there to get a statement.'

'If she sticks with it,' Jesse said, 'arrest the husband, read him his rights. Call the DA's office.'

'You going to go see the people at – ' She looked down at her notebook again. ' – Development Associates of Boston?'

'Yeah.'

'If this Snyder thing gets complicated, I'll call you.'

'Molly, you run this station better than I do,' Jesse said.

'I know,' Molly said. 'But the sexist bastards made you chief.'

'Oh,' Jesse said. 'Yeah.'

26

Development Associates of Boston was in the South End, not far from the Cyclorama, one flight down, with a plate-glass window looking out onto the cement stairway. The room had been recycled from whatever it used to be. The walls were old brick and the beams had been exposed and sandblasted. The young man at the reception desk had curly black hair and big blue eyes. He was very good-looking.

'Hi,' Jesse said, 'the boss in?'

'Do you have an appointment?' the young man said.

Jesse showed him his badge. The young man looked at it closely.

'What police department is that?' he said.

'Paradise,' Jesse said. 'North Shore.'

'And what was it about?'

'I'll talk to the boss.'

'Mr. Fish never sees anyone without an appointment,' the young man said.

'And your name is?' Jesse said.

'Alan Garner.' The young man widened his eyes and smiled again. 'Is your interest personal or professional?'

Jesse put his badge away.

'Alan,' Jesse said, 'we can do this easy, or we can do it hard. Easy is I go in and sit with your boss and discuss my case. Hard is I go get a Boston cop and we bring your boss in for questioning.'

The young man smiled at Jesse again. No hard feelings.

'I'll talk to Mr. Fish,' he said, and went through a curtained archway.

Jesse looked around. There were framed prints of sailboats, and a hanging lamp with a dark green shade. The furniture was the kind of bleached oak that was bought secondhand in Europe and refinished and sold at a large profit in the USA. Mr. Fish. The name was familiar. It had come up in a case Jesse had when he first came to Paradise. Not a common name.

The good-looking young man came back into the room and smiled again at Jesse.

'Surprise, surprise,' he said.

'Mr. Fish will see me,' Jesse said.

'You bet,' the young man said, and gestured Jesse in.

A tall, lean man with a shaved head and long, graceful fingers sat behind a big oak table in a room that was just like the anteroom but bigger.

'I'm Gino Fish,' he said.

It had to be him, Jesse thought, *how many Gino Fishes are there?*

'Jesse Stone.'

Against the wall to Gino's left and Jesse's right sat a compact man with an expressionless face. Jesse could almost feel the force of his meaningless stare.

'And you are?' Jesse said.

'My associate,' Fish said, 'Vinnie Morris.'

'I'm looking for a girl,' Jesse said, 'named Billie Bishop.'

'And why are you looking here?' Fish said.

'She told someone she could be reached at this phone number.'

Fish stared at Jesse for a long moment before he spoke.

'Vinnie, do we know anyone named Billie Bishop?'

Vinnie shook his head.

'I guess we don't,' Fish said.

'You have any explanation for the phone number?'

'None.'

'What does Development Associates do?' Jesse asked.

'Development and marketing,' Gino said.

'Development and marketing of what?' Jesse said.

'Our best interests,' Gino said.

'Do you remember developing and marketing a little something with a guy named JoJo Genest?'

'No.'

'Hasty Hathaway?'

'No.'

'Gino,' Jesse said. 'I'm not sure you're leveling with me.'

'Why wouldn't I level with you, Jesse?' Gino said. 'We've been close personal friends for what, five or six minutes?'

'Of course,' Jesse said.

He put a business card on Gino's desk.

'You think of anything, give me a ringy dingy,' Jesse said.

'You bet,' Gino said. 'Nice of you to stop by.'

Vinnie had been looking at Jesse with nothing in his eyes since Jesse had entered.

Jesse turned and shot Vinnie with his forefinger. Vinnie had no reaction as Jesse walked back out through the draped arch.

27

Jesse sat in a cubicle in the Organized Crime Unit in the new Boston Police headquarters and talked with a detective sergeant named Brian Kelly.

'Bobby Doyle over in District Thirteen told me you were the man to talk to,' Jesse said.

'He still in youth service?' Kelly said.

'Yes.'

'I used to work over there in Area C,' Kelly said. 'Whaddya need?'

He was about Jesse's size with thick black hair cut short. He looked in shape.

'Gino Fish,' Jesse said.

Kelly rocked back in his swivel chair and paused for a moment.

'Ahh,' Kelly said. 'Gino.'

Jesse nodded.

'OCU spends a lot of time thinking about Gino Fish,' Kelly said.

'What can you tell me?' Jesse said.

'How long you been chief out there?' Kelly said.

'Four years.'

'Work your way up?'

Jesse smiled.

'Down, I think,' Jesse said. 'I was in L.A. working homicide. I got fired for drinking on the job, which sobered me up some, and I sort of resurfaced in Paradise.'

'What's the deal with Gino?' Kelly said.

Jesse knew he had passed.

'There was a floater in the lake,' Jesse said. 'Shot once behind the right ear and weighted. Body pulled loose from the weight and surfaced.'

'Execution?'

'I would guess,' Jesse said. 'She was a kid named Billie Bishop. Runaway, and the last place she ran away from, she gave Gino's phone number as a forwarding address.'

'She was with Sister Mary John,' Kelly said.

'Yes.'

'Which is how you ran into Bobby Doyle.'

'Yes.'

'I didn't know Bobby knew about Gino,' Kelly said.

'He didn't. I did. His name came up a few years ago in a case I was on.'

'In Paradise?'

'Yep.'

'Mean streets,' Kelly said.

Jesse smiled.

'So,' he said, 'you know any reason a fifteen-year-old girl would be giving people Gino's number?'

'Gino's into a lot of things,' Kelly said. 'None of them pleasant.' He grinned. 'But girls are not usually one of them.'

'I picked that up,' Jesse said.

'So she wouldn't be for his own use,' Kelly said. 'There'd have to be a profit motive. Kid come from money?'

'Not that kind,' Jesse said.

'So …'

'So sex.'

'Gino hasn't got much background in prostitution,' Kelly said.

'Because he wouldn't?'

'There's nothing Gino wouldn't,' Kelly said. 'He just hasn't.'

'How about Vinnie Morris?'

Kelly shook his head. 'He wouldn't.'

'He a shooter?' Jesse said.

'They say he shoots clays with a handgun.'

'Nobody can do that,' Jesse said.

Kelly shrugged.

'He's a shooter,' Kelly said. 'Clay pigeons, people, don't make any difference to Vinnie.'

'But?'

'But,' Kelly shook his head. 'You know how some of these guys are. There's stuff he won't do.'

'Like prostitution?'

'Like that. Like dope.'

'So what's he do for Gino?'

'Bodyguard, enforcement. Gino needs to threaten somebody, Vinnie's the threat. People threaten Gino, Vinnie's the response.'

'How far from the street is Gino?' Jesse asked.

'Far. City used to be run by a guy named Joe Broz, but he got old, and his kid wasn't up to it. So things got divided up. The Feds put the Italians out of business. Tony Marcus runs Roxbury and part of Dorchester. The Burkes have the Irish neighborhoods like Southie. Fast Eddie Lee has Chinatown. Gino's pretty much got what's left: South End, Back Bay.'

'So if Gino's an executive, how does he come in contact with a street kid like Billie Bishop?'

'Maybe you start at the other end,' Kelly said. 'Who likes fifteen-year-old girls?'

'That knows Gino Fish,' Jesse said.

'And maybe has a connection to Paradise,' Kelly said.

'That Gino likes?' Jesse said.

'That Gino can use.'

28

The room was empty of ornament. Just a gray metal desk, an extra chair, and a swivel chair with a man sitting in it behind the desk. The man was white, entirely bald, clean-shaven. He wore a white shirt buttoned to the neck and a pair of pale blue jeans. The shirt and jeans were starched and pressed. His face was healthy-looking. His teeth were very white. His fingernails gleamed. The man's name was Dix.

Jesse sat in the extra chair.

'My name is Jesse Stone,' he said. 'My ex-wife says she's talked to you.'

'She did,' Dix said.

'You used to be a cop.'

'Until I gave it up to be a drunk.'

'What pushed your button?' Jesse said.

'My boozer button?'

'You know,' Jesse said, 'the precipitating event.'

Dix laughed. Jesse noticed that Dix's hands lay perfectly still, one on top of the other on the desk in front of him.

'Booze,' Dix said.

'Booze?'

'I was a drinker of opportunity,' Dix said. 'As soon as I could get booze, I did.'

'I was all right until my wife left.'

'No, you weren't. Even if you were sober. You were a drunk waiting to happen.'

Jesse was silent for a time. Dix waited. He seemed ready to wait for the rest of eternity. There was nothing hurried in him.

'Lot of wives leave a lot of husbands,' Jesse said.

Dix nodded.

'Not all the husbands have a drinking problem.'

Dix nodded again.

'You married?' Jesse said.

'My wife left me because I was a drunk,' Dix said. 'By the time I got sober she was with somebody else.'

'Tough.'

'I earned it,' Dix said. 'Like they say, if you can't do the time, don't do the crime.'

'Booze kill the job, too?'

'Yes.'

'How'd you get sober?'

'I stopped drinking,' Dix said.

'That's the secret?'

'You're a drunk because you drink,' Dix said. 'Don't drink, you're not a drunk.'

'You don't believe in addiction?'

'Sure I do. I was addicted. Still am. But that's an explanation. You want to stop drinking, pal, you have to do more than explain it.'

Jesse smiled a little.

'You're a cold bastard, aren't you,' he said.

'Stopping is cold bastard work,' Dix said. 'Ever been to a shrink?'

'Not till now.'

'Lotta people go to the shrink. They discover their childhood. They understand why they do what they do. And they say, "Oh boy, now I understand why I'm such a full-bore blue-blooded asshole." And they think they're cured.'

'But they aren't,' Jesse said.

'They're halfway,' Dix said. 'The trick is to stop being a full-bore blue-blooded asshole.'

'I sense a parable,' Jesse said.

Dix smiled. 'You need will as well as understanding.'

'There's the rub,' Jesse said.

'Yep. There's the rub,' Dix said.

'Can you help?'

'What am I, another pretty face? Of course I can help you. But I can't stop you. You got to find a reason for that.'

'Like a higher power?' Jesse said.

'Like not getting your ass shot because you're drunk while serving and protecting,' Dix said.

'So what do we do?'

'We talk,' Dix said. 'We think about where you are and how you got there. Sometimes I offer advice.'

'Like what?'

'Like drink a lot of orange juice. Your body starts to crave sugar when you give up booze.'

'Why juice?'

'Because it's better for you than candy bars and tonic,' Dix said.

'For that I'm paying a hundred and fifty an hour?'

'A hundred and sixty-five an hour,' Dix said. 'I'm here all the time. You can call me anytime. You can stop by at 3:00 A.M. if you want. We can talk. We can sort out the things you tell yourself. And we can agree once again that the way to stop is to stop.'

'And I'm doing this why?'

'You tell me,' Dix said.

'I need to stop drinking.'

Dix nodded.

'Jenn tell you about me?'

Dix nodded.

'This job, in Paradise, is the last stop. I get off the bus here and where do I go?'

'Freud says the things that matter most to people are love and work,' Dix said.

'I don't want to be zero for two.'

'I don't know where it will lead,' Dix said. 'But I've talked with Jenn, and the connection between you is very powerful.'

'You're saying maybe I could be two for two?'

'I'm saying you do what you can. Jenn is up to Jenn. But the work is up to you.'

'I can do the work,' Jesse said.

'If you're sober.'

'And Jenn?'

'Jenn will do what she will do,' Dix said. 'All you can do is be sober.'

'And staying sober helps the work and the work helps the staying sober.'

'Can't hurt,' Dix said.

Again they sat quietly in the unadorned room. Dix remained motionless.

'That's what you're doing,' Jesse said.

Dix didn't answer.

'You stay sober by helping people stay sober,' Jesse said.

'See, you learned something already.'

Jesse thought about it. He laughed.

'I need a drink,' he said.

'Me too,' Dix said.

'But you won't.'

'Nope.'

They were silent for a long time. Jesse could hear his breath going in and out. Dix didn't move. The steadiness of his gaze was implacable.

'And if I can't quit?' Jesse said finally.

Dix waited a moment before he answered.

'Then,' he said, 'you're fucked.'

29

Jesse sat in the sunroom off the front parlor of the house in Swampscott and talked with Hank and Sandy Bishop.

'The dead girl we found in Paradise is your daughter Elinor,' Jesse said.

Sandy Bishop's mouth was thin with denial. Her husband seemed to have disappeared behind the blank facade of his face.

'That can't be,' Sandy Bishop said.

'I'm sorry,' Jesse said. 'But it is. We know it's Billie, and we know Billie is your daughter.'

Hank Bishop's face seemed to grow tighter. Sandy's pretty cheerleader face became more disapproving. Jesse felt as if he had misbehaved and she were going to scold him. Jesse waited. Hank Bishop opened his mouth and closed it. He looked at his wife. She continued to gaze at Jesse, the disapproval in her face unflinching. Jesse waited. Hank's breathing was audible. He seemed short of breath. He tried to speak.

'We …'

Sandy raised her right hand sharply as if she were tossing something away.

'Billie was lost to us,' she said, 'a long time ago.'

The only thing Jesse could hear in her voice was the same disapproval that had shown in her face.

'How long?'

'She ran away from us at the end of the school year, but she had left us in every other way long before that.'

'You didn't get along?' Jesse said.

'She didn't get along. We have two other daughters. We get along with them. Emily is at Mount Holyoke. Carla is captain of her soccer team.'

'Do you know anyone she might have been with?' Jesse said.

'No.'

Jesse looked at Hank Bishop. He didn't speak.

Jesse said, 'Any thoughts, Mr. Bishop?'

Bishop shook his head.

'Do either of you know anyone named Gino Fish?' Jesse said.

Sandy Bishop said, 'No.'

Jesse looked at her husband. Hank Bishop was looking at the gray-green carpeting between his feet. He shook his head.

'Vinnie Morris?'

'No.'

'Development Associates of Boston?'

'No.'

'When she ran away, do you know where she went?'

'No.'

'Could I get a list of her friends?'

'She never brought her friends home,' Sandy Bishop said. 'Except Hooker Royce, and he didn't last long.'

'Do you know why?'

'She couldn't hold on to a boyfriend any better than she did anything else,' Sandy said.

'Do you have any theory about how she died, or why?'

'No,' Sandy said. 'And we don't want to keep talking about it. We mourned Elinor's death long before this. We don't want to go through that pain again.'

'I understand,' Jesse said.

'No. I don't think you do,' Sandy said. 'But whether you do or don't, all we ask is that you leave us alone. We have nothing else to say.'

Jesse looked at Hank Bishop. Hank was still looking at the carpet. Jesse closed his notebook and stood. He tucked the notebook and the Bic ballpoint into his jacket pocket.

'Thank you for your time,' Jesse said.

Neither of the Bishops said anything. Jesse walked through the color-coordinated pastel living room to the front hall and opened the front door and went out and closed the door behind him.

Outside it was a bright summer day flavored with the faint smell of ocean drifting up from a beach he couldn't see.

The female of the species, Jesse thought.

30

Vivian Snyder came into Jesse's office with Molly. Her left arm was in a cast. She had two black eyes and Jesse could tell that there was packing in her nose. Jesse got to his feet.

'Sit down, Mrs. Snyder,' he said.

When she had eased into a chair, Vivian Snyder looked at Molly.

'I don't want her here,' Vivian said.

Jesse nodded to Molly. She went out, leaving the door open. Jesse was quiet. Vivian looked uncomfortable in her chair. She looked around the office. File cabinets, coffeemaker, computer, window overlooking the parking area in front of the fire station.

'You married?' Vivian said.

'No.'

'Ever been married?'

'Yes.'

Vivian nodded as if what he had said were significant. Jesse waited.

'The bastard has been hitting me for years,' Vivian said.

'Why do you stay?' Jesse said.

'I'm Catholic. I'm not supposed to get divorced.'

'Have you talked with your priest?'

'No. I didn't want nobody to know.'

'But you're talking with me?'

'You know anyway.'

Jesse nodded. Outside Jesse's window some firemen were polishing one of the trucks. Their voices sounded happy.

'I don't want a divorce,' Vivian said.

She was looking at her right hand, as if she were checking the polish on her fingernails.

'We been together a long time,' she said. 'We went to high school together.'

'Hard to walk away from that,' Jesse said.

'He didn't used to hit me.'

'Is it booze?' Jesse said.

'Mostly. He usually won't hit me unless he's drinking.'

'Any kids in the house?'

'No. We never had kids.'

Outside the window one of the firemen whooped with laughter.

'You want to bring charges against your husband?' Jesse said.

'I don't know what to do,' Vivian said.

Jesse was still. She'd get to it.

'I'm fifty-three years old, and I drunk too much for twenty years, and I'm fat and stupid and I look like shit.'

Jesse made a neutral gesture with one hand.

'I got no kids,' Vivian said.

Jesse nodded.

'I got no money. I got no education.'

Jesse nodded.

'Last job I had was waitressing at a pancake house in Lakeville.'

Jesse stayed still and waited.

'I lose Jerry, what the fuck have I got?' she said, and began to cry.

'A rock and a hard place,' Jesse said.

Molly appeared at the open door and looked in. Jesse shook his head slightly and Molly went away. Vivian sat with her head down and cried aloud. After a time she got her breathing under control and raised her face.

'Maybe you could talk to him,' she said.

'I could do that,' Jesse said.

'I don't know what else to do,' Vivian said.

'You and your husband ever been in counseling?'

'You mean a shrink?'

'Yeah.'

'I'm not talking to nobody,' she said.

'Except me,' Jesse said.

'Shrinks are all crazy anyway,' she said.

She was crying again. Jesse sighed and nodded slowly.

'Okay,' he said. 'I'll talk to him.'

31

'This is Molly Crane,' Jesse said. 'Lilly Summers.'

'Nice to meet you,' Molly said.

'And you,' Lilly said.

She nodded at Jesse.

'How is he to work for?'

'Needs a lot of attention,' Molly said.

'He does,' Lilly said, 'doesn't he?'

They walked past the desk and into the corridor. To the left was Jesse's office. Straight ahead was the squad room. To the right was the line of four holding cells.

'I don't think I've ever seen a jail cell,' Lilly said. 'They don't look very tempting.'

'They're not supposed to be,' Jesse said.

The squad room had a long pine table in the center. It was

yellow with shellac. There was an empty pizza box on it, some empty cardboard coffee cups, and a carton half full of donuts.

There were two cubicles on the back wall. There was a computer set up in each.

'Looks like the faculty lounge,' Lilly said. 'This where you gather the men to solve crimes?'

'When they're not eating,' Jesse said.

'Where do you keep guns and things?'

'There's an equipment closet off the squad room.'

He held the door to his office open as Lilly went in.

'So this is where you rule,' she said.

'And read the paper,' Jesse said.

Lilly walked around the small office. She picked up Jenn's picture from Jesse's desk.

'This her?'

'Yes.'

'She looks familiar.'

'She's the weather girl on Channel Three.'

'I think you're supposed to say "Weather Woman."'

'I think so,' Jesse said.

Lilly looked at the picture another long moment before she put it back on Jesse's desk.

'I wish she weren't so damned good-looking,' she said.

'Me, too,' Jesse said. 'Want some coffee?'

'Sure.'

Jesse poured two cups and gave her one. She sat across from his desk and sipped it.

'Have you found out about Billie Bishop?' Lilly said.

'The dead girl is Billie Bishop,' Jesse said.

'Oh dear,' Lilly said. 'You're sure.'

'I am.'

Lilly had on a dark blue warm-up suit. Her hair was caught back with a blue headband.

'Have you told the parents?'

'Yes.'

Jesse had on jeans and a corduroy jacket.

'How were they?'

'Very unusual,' Jesse said.

'Grief?'

'I'm not sure. The father, I think so. The mother? Maybe not.'

'Are you serious?'

'The mother was maybe relieved,' Jesse said.

'My God.'

'Whatever else is going on in that family,' Jesse said, 'it's the mother that controls it.'

'I don't think I ever met her,' Lilly said.

'I've had to tell a number of people that someone has died,' Jesse said. 'She's not like anyone else.'

'What are you going to do?'

'We have a name in Boston. I have Suit going through the Internet, see if he can find anything that this name would have in common with Billie, or Paradise, or Swampscott.'

'Suit?'

'Officer Simpson. We call him Suitcase.'

'After the ballplayer,' Lilly said.

'Very good.'

Lilly nodded. She stood and walked to the file cabinet and picked up a baseball glove.

'Is this your glove?'

'Yes.'

She read the label on the wrist strap.

'Rawlings,' she said. 'Is it a good one?'

'Yes.'

'Have you always had it?'

'Since the Dodgers signed me.'

'Do you still use it when you play softball?'

'Sure. That's why the pocket is so big.'

Lilly nodded, looking at the glove.

'I'd love to see you play some night.'

Jesse looked at the calendar on his desk next to Jenn's picture.

'We play Thursday night,' he said. 'Game starts at six.'

Lilly nodded. She put the glove back on top of the file cabinet.

'How about Molly?' she said.

'How about her?'

'You and she? Anything?'

'No. Molly's married, got kids in school.'

'That doesn't always prevent things,' Lilly said.

'It does in this case.'

'What's her husband do?'

'He's a carpenter. Works in the Rucker Boatyard.'

'Does she ever do anything but cover the front desk?' Lilly said.

'Sure.'

'So she's not just a secretary with a gun?'

'No. She likes the day shift and she likes to be in the station so her kids can reach her if they need to.'

'Couldn't they reach their father – at the boatyard?'

'They can.'

'Fathers are as responsible for their children as mothers.'

'That would be my guess,' Jesse said.

She smiled at him.

'You're pretty hard to argue with, aren't you?'

'I think so,' Jesse said.

Lilly got up again and walked past Jesse's desk and stared down at the fire trucks parked outside the station.

'I've never had sex in a police station,' she said.

Jesse smiled. 'Me either.'

'Does anyone ever have sex in one of the cells?' Lilly said.

'Not to my knowledge.'

'Maybe somebody should,' Lilly said.

'I don't think so.'

'Would you dare?' Lilly said. Her voice was bubbly with humor and something else.

'No.'

'Scaredy-cat?' Lilly said.

'That's me,' Jesse said.

'I've always had a fantasy of sex in some public place.'

'You have a hidden side,' Jesse said.

Lilly turned from the window and looked directly at him. The humor and something else in her voice glistened in her eyes.

'I do,' she said.

Jesse didn't say anything.

'Does it bother you?' Lilly said.

'No,' Jesse said. 'I like it.'

'But you wouldn't make love to me in a jail cell?'

'Not one of mine,' Jesse said.

Again Lilly looked straight at him. 'How about your office?'

'Can't,' Jesse said.

The sound was still in her voice and the look was still in her eyes, but there might have been the tinge of annoyance in both.

'Because?'

'Because I don't want to be caught.'

'What's the worst that could happen?'

'It would embarrass me, and the department,' Jesse said.

'School principals aren't supposed to do that kind of thing either. It would embarrass me, too. But the risk is part of the fun.'

'I like you. I like to have sex with you. But this is what I have. I'm divorced from the only woman I seem able to love. I am trying not to drink. I can't play professional baseball like I was supposed to. All I can be is a cop, and this is my last chance at that.'

'And you can't jeopardize it.'

Jesse smiled. He felt himself relax. She understood.

'No. I can't. Not for fun.'

'Will Jenn always be the only woman you're able to love?'

'I don't know. She is so far.'

Lilly sighed, and smiled.

'Well,' she said. 'I guess I'll just hang around and see.'

'You can't count on me changing,' Jesse said.

'Maybe not. But I can count on you to fuck my brains out, can't I?'

'Absolutely,' Jesse said.

32

Jesse had breakfast with Lilly before she went home, and he was late coming to work. It was a deeply still summer morning that you can only get in a small town. Cloudless. Hot. Silent. As if everything was going to live forever.

'Suit's in the squad room,' Molly said when Jesse came into the station. 'He says to come see him.'

Simpson was at one of the computers.

'I got a hit,' he said when Jesse came into the room.

'On what?' Jesse said.

'Gino Fish. I got a connection with Paradise.'

'Which is?'

'This'll knock your socks off,' Simpson said.

'Sure,' Jesse said.

'Norman Shaw,' Simpson said. 'How about that?'

'Knocks my socks off,' Jesse said. 'What's the connection?'

'Article in the *Globe* five years back,' Simpson said. 'Shaw was going to write a book about Gino and they were going to make a movie out of it.'

'You print it out?'

'Yeah.'

Simpson handed Jesse a sheet of paper.

'Anything else?' Jesse said.

'Not that helps us. He did ten years at Walpole for killing a guy with a straight razor.'

'Nice,' Jesse said.

'Was one of the people they covered when they did that big spotlight thing on organized crime.'

'Anything about girls?'

'Says in here he is alleged to be gay.'

'I know. Anything about prostitution?'

'Nothing specific. Just says he's the alleged boss of all criminal activity in Downtown and Back Bay.'

'Well,' Jesse said and gestured with the printout. 'I'll take this. You print out the rest and put it on my desk.'

'Print out all of it?'

'Yep.'

'There's 5,145 entries for Gino Fish.'

'Most of them are for fish markets, or tropical fish collectors, or sportsmen or other guys named Fish, or Papa Gino's pizza,' Jesse said. 'Internet's not too selective.'

'Don't I know it,' Simpson said.

'So just print out the ones about Gino Fish, and don't duplicate.'

'I hate the internet,' Simpson said.

'Information highway,' Jesse said.

'Mostly bullshit highway,' Simpson said.

'No one ever said crimebusting was pretty,' Jesse said.

33

When she opened the front door Joni Shaw said, 'Oh, oh, the fuzz.'

'May I come in?'

'Are you planning to search the place?' Joni Shaw said.

'No, I just want to talk.'

She smiled widely at him and stepped away from the door.

The entry hall of Norman Shaw's big house was twenty feet wide with a curved staircase to the second floor. At the turn a full-length window was full of sunlight. To the right of the front door there was an umbrella stand made from the lower part of an elephant's leg, and a dark wine-colored Persian rug lay across the width of the hall at the foot of the stairs.

'Let's sit in the atrium,' Joni Shaw said.

She led Jesse through a room lined with bookshelves and scattered with heavy nineteenth-century furniture, into a glass atrium where the ocean was visible a hundred yards below, tossing spray toward the house as it broke on the rocks. Jesse sat on the end of a green leather chaise.

'Coffee?' Joni Shaw said. 'A drink?'

'Coffee would be nice,' Jesse said.

'That will make it a social call,' Joni Shaw said.

'Sure,' Jesse said.

Joni Shaw was dressed in black shorts and a white silk tee shirt that stopped short of her waist so that her stomach showed. An Asian woman brought coffee. Jesse added cream and sugar and drank some.

'Is your husband at home?' Jesse said.

'Oh, damn,' she said. 'I thought you'd come calling on me.'

Jesse smiled and didn't say anything.

'Norman is working,' Joni Shaw said. 'He works every morning in his study with the door locked.'

'Here in the house,' Jesse said.

'Yes. But it might as well be on Mars,' Joni Shaw said. 'He is simply not here when he's working.'

'Well, maybe you can help me,' Jesse said.

'I hope so,' Joni Shaw said.

Jesse noticed that everything she said seemed to imply something more.

'Do you know a man named Gino Fish?'

'The gangster?'

'Un-huh.'

'Sure.'

'Talk about him a little,' Jesse said.

'Why do you ask?'

'His name has come up in a case I'm working on,' Jesse said.

'Oh my, are we suspects?'

'No. I'm just looking for help.'

Joni Shaw was sitting on the couch across from Jesse, with one leg on the couch so that he could see the inside of her thigh. She sipped her coffee, looking at Jesse over the rim of her cup.

'Aren't we all,' she said.

Jesse waited. Joni Shaw let him wait.

'Gino Fish?' Jesse said after he had waited long enough.

'You may remember that about five years ago one of Norman's books was being made into a movie, here, in Boston.'

Jesse nodded as if he remembered. Five years ago he'd been in L.A., on the cops, still with Jenn.

'Norman was an executive producer on the movie. He didn't really have to do anything, it was just a title, extra money. Gino used to visit the set. He knew some of the crew. Then when we had some trouble with the union, Gino was very helpful.'

'How nice,' Jesse said.

Without leaving the couch, Joni Shaw leaned forward and poured him some more coffee. Very flexible.

'Oh,' Joni said, 'I don't doubt that Gino has done some terrible things. But he's a very interesting person.'

Jesse nodded.

'I try to make my own judgments of people,' Joni said, 'and so does Norman. Gino has been very nice to us, and good fun at a party.'

'So he's become a friend?'

'I guess you could say that,' Joni Shaw said. 'Not perhaps the first circle of intimacy, but certainly more than just an acquaintance.'

She made 'first circle of intimacy' sound seductive.

'Do you know anyone named Bishop?' Jesse said.

'I don't think so. Is he involved in your case?'

'When's the last time you saw Gino?' Jesse said.

'Oh … two, no, three, weeks ago. In fact he was at the party where you were going to arrest us.'

'Anyone with him?'

Joni smiled.

'A very good-looking young man,' she said.

'And, I wasn't going to arrest you,' Jesse said.

Joni Shaw drank a small sip of her coffee, holding the cup in both hands, like in a television commercial, and looking at Jesse.

'Oh, well,' she said. 'Can't blame a girl for hoping.'

34

Jesse sat beside Brian Kelly with the windows open in an unmarked gray Ford that belonged to the Boston Police Department. They were a half block up Tremont Street from Development Associates of Boston. It was a hot, clear, day.

'OCU got no surveillance on Gino Fish?' Jesse said.

'Nope. He's down the list,' Kelly said.

'How come?' Jesse said.

'Everything in his part of the city is quiet,' Kelly said. 'Commissioner likes it.'

'How come it's so quiet?'

'Gino's a good administrator,' Kelly said. 'There's not much street crime on Gino's turf. Commissioner hates street crime.'

Jesse looked at the brick-and-brownstone rehab that was spread over the South End like brocade.

'Doesn't look like a street-crime neighborhood.'

'It isn't anymore.'

'And Gino cleaned it up?'

'Not really. Economics did that. But Gino keeps it that way,' Kelly said. 'Him and Vinnie.'

'So I guess you people aren't going to be a big help.'

'Can't give you manpower. Happy to offer advice.'

'Why should you be different?' Jesse said.

'You spare anybody?'

'I got twelve people,' Jesse said.

'How are they at covert surveillance?'

'Not much call for that in Paradise,' Jesse said.

A black Lexus sedan with tinted windows pulled up in front

of Development Associates and sat at the curb, its motor idling.

'This is exciting,' Kelly said.

The car sat for five minutes and then Vinnie Morris came out of the office and up the steps and stood outside the car. In a moment Gino Fish came out with the good-looking young man. The young man locked the office door, and they came up the steps together and got into the backseat of the Lexus. The door closed. The Lexus pulled away from the curb.

'You want to follow them?' Kelly said.

'Alone?'

'We got nobody else,' Kelly said.

'I don't want to let him know,' Jesse said. 'We can't tail him in one car.'

The Lexus turned up Dartmouth Street and disappeared. On the sidewalk in front of the office, Vinnie Morris fiddled with a Walkman on his belt for a moment, then put on the earphones and turned and walked up Tremont Street with his hands in his pockets.

'You want to commit an illegal burglary?' Kelly said.

'Not yet,' Jesse said. 'Place is probably alarmed.'

'Probably,' Kelly said. 'You got a plan?'

'I don't want to tip him,' Jesse said. 'I want him conducting business as usual.'

'And?'

'And I guess all I can do is come in every day and watch him. See what develops.'

Kelly's hands were resting on the steering wheel. He drummed his fingers for a moment.

Kelly said, 'I'll help you when I can.'

'We do and it's your collar,' Jesse said.

'Whose ever collar it is, it would be a pleasure to haul him off.'

'And, it'll be our secret,' Jesse said.

'Meaning?'

'Meaning your captain doesn't find out you're cheating on

him. And nobody else on the job knows I'm chasing Gino.'

'You think he's got a cop on his tab?' Kelly said.

'What do you think?'

'I think guys like Gino usually do.'

'That's what I think, too,' Jesse said.

35

When Jerry Snyder came out of the car dealership where he worked, Jesse, in jeans and a gray tee shirt, was leaning on the fender of the aging Ford Explorer in which he had driven east when he left L.A.

'Whaddya want?' Snyder said. 'You ain't even a cop in this town.'

'We need to talk,' Jesse said.

'I don't want to talk with you, pal.'

'Why would you?' Jesse said, and opened the door on the passenger side of the Explorer. 'Get in.'

Jesse's tee shirt was not tucked in. It hung down over his belt, partially hiding the gun on his right hip.

'Are you arresting me?'

'Hell no,' Jesse said.

'Then I don't have to go.'

He held the door open. Another salesman walked by with a customer. Both of them looked uneasily at Jesse and Snyder.

'Sure you don't,' Jesse said. 'We can talk about domestic violence right here.'

The salesman and the customer looked again and quickly away, trying to act as if they hadn't heard.

'Jesus Christ,' Snyder said.

Jesse still held the car door open. Snyder looked around, and then at Jesse, and got into the car. Jesse closed the door and went around and got in and started the car.

'You wanna get me fired?' Snyder said.

Jesse didn't answer.

'Where we going?'

'Someplace where we can talk, and you won't get fired,' Jesse said.

'I ain't done nothing wrong,' Snyder said.

They drove south on Route 1, and crossed the Paradise town line. Jesse pulled the car off onto the little cul-de-sac near the lake where Billie Bishop had been found. He turned off the engine and took out his gun. Snyder's eyes widened.

'Open your mouth,' Jesse said.

'What the hell are you doing?' Snyder said.

Jesse tapped him on the upper lip with the muzzle of the handgun.

'Open,' Jesse said.

Snyder opened his mouth and Jesse put the gun barrel into it. Jesse didn't say anything. Snyder tried to swallow. Behind them the traffic went routinely by on Route 1. The hot damp smell of the lake came in through the open windows of the Explorer. Jesse looked at Snyder without expression.

'This is the only chance I'm going to give you,' Jesse said after a time.

Snyder was breathing in small gasps.

'You hit your wife again and I'm going to kill you,' Jesse said.

Again Snyder tried to swallow and failed. He raised both hands in front of his chest, palms toward Jesse. Jesse held the gun steady. His face was expressionless. Below them, down the hill toward the lake, a group of insects made a keening hum.

'You understand that?' Jesse said.

Snyder nodded his head maybe an inch.

'You believe me?'

Snyder nodded slightly as if it hurt to move his head.

Jesse took the gun from Snyder's mouth and put it back in its holster.

'Get out of the car,' Jesse said.

Snyder got out.

'Close the door,' Jesse said.

Snyder closed the door. Jesse started his engine, put the car in gear and drove away.

36

Lilly came down to the lakeside one evening to watch Jesse play. Though it was still bright, the lights were on. The players gathered in shorts and sweats and tee shirts and tank tops and baseball caps on backward. All of them had expensive gloves, and the talk among them was the same talk, she thought, that Cap Anson had heard, or Cobb, or Ruth, or Mickey Mantle: insulting, self-deprecating, valued for its originality less than for its tradition, like the ancient ballad singers she'd heard of, rearranging the same phrases to create something new. The music was the same. Beloved teammates. Beloved adversaries. Celebrating the same ritual, together on a summer evening. She felt entirely separate from this. She understood it, but she knew she'd never feel it. If there were real differences between the genders, she thought, she was observing one of them.

Looking at the game, her eyes were drawn to Jesse. It wasn't just because of their intimacy, she was pretty sure. It was the way he moved. Among twenty or more men who all valued the same thing, Jesse seemed most to embody it.

It was darkening after the game. Jesse and Lilly walked across the outfield toward the parking lot. The coolers were open. The beer was out. The cans were popped. The bright malty smell of the beer rode gently on the evening air. The men smelled of clean sweat. Jesse took two beers from a cooler and opened them and handed one to Lilly. She took it though she didn't like beer much.

'I don't belong here,' Lilly said.

Jesse smiled.

'Can she play short?' someone said. 'We need someone, bad, to play short.'

Jesse held up his hands, all five fingers spread.

'Five for five,' Jesse said.

He walked with Lilly across the parking lot toward his car. He had his glove under his left arm, and the open beer in his right.

'Don't you want to stay and drink beer with your friends?' Lilly said. 'I could meet you later.'

'No,' Jesse said. 'I'd rather drink beer with you.'

She liked that. They sat in his car in the quiet, drinking their beer.

'You got a hit every time,' Lilly said.

Jesse nodded.

'People hit eight hundred in this league,' Jesse said. 'Nobody's throwing a major-league slider up there.'

The beer was very cold. One of her husbands had insisted on drinking it at room temperature, claiming that you could experience the beer's full complexity. Lilly found it more tolerable cold.

'You're being modest,' she said.

'No,' Jesse said. 'I'm being accurate. I'm supposed to go five for five. I was a professional ballplayer.'

'And the other players never were.'

'No.'

'And professionals beat amateurs.'

'Every time,' Jesse said. 'You want another beer?'

'God no,' Lilly said.

'You don't like beer.'

'No.'

'We don't have to stay here,' Jesse said. 'We could go someplace and get something you like.'

'I like it here.'

'Okay.'

Jesse got out of the car and got another beer and brought it back.

Someone yelled, 'You doing something bad in that car, Jesse?'

Jesse got back in the front seat and closed the door. He

drank some beer. It didn't have the jolt that scotch did, and it took longer. But it had enough.

'Do you feel the same way about being a policeman?' Lilly said.

'As?'

'As being a ballplayer,' Lilly said. 'You know – professionals and amateurs?'

'Yes.'

'And you're a professional policeman.'

'I am.'

'And it matters to you.'

'Yes.'

Someone had turned the field lights off. They could see the moon at the low arc of the horizon. They were quiet. There was something surprisingly romantic about sitting in a silent car with the windows down on a summer night. *Maybe the memory of going parking*, Lilly thought, *memory of the uncertain groping in parked cars when everyone first had their license*. It had all been starting then. She had not contemplated, then, being twice divorced at forty, living alone in an uninteresting condominium.

'Is the police work more important than Jenn?'

'No.'

'Maybe it should be.'

Jesse drank the rest of his beer.

'Because?'

'Because you can control the police work,' Lilly said. 'At least some of it.'

'And I can't control Jenn.'

'Nobody can control anybody,' Lilly said.

'I don't want to control her, I just want to love her.'

Lilly smiled in the darkness. She thought of all the psychotherapy that had escorted her through two bad marriages. *Shrinks must get bored*, she thought. *Always the same illusions. Always the same mistakes.*

'You can do that now,' she said to Jesse. 'What you want is

102

for her to love you. You have to trust her to do that.'

Jesse stared out through the windshield at the opaque surface of the darkening lake.

'I'm not sure I can,' he said after a time.

'That's the bitch of it,' Lilly said.

The parking lot was getting empty. Most of the beer was gone, and the Boys of Evening were drifting back to home and wives and children. Back to adulthood. None of them would have given that up to play ball forever in the twilight. But all of them were grateful for the evenings when they could.

Beside him in the front seat Lilly said, 'I feel as if we ought to neck.'

'If we can do it without breaking a rib on the storage compartment between us,' Jesse said.

'When you were seventeen that wouldn't have bothered you,' Lilly said.

'When I was seventeen I didn't have an apartment to neck in.'

'And now you do.'

'And now I do.'

'Well then,' Lilly said. 'Lets go there.'

'And neck?'

'For starters,' she said.

37

Jesse, out of uniform, sat in his own car on Tremont Street and watched the front door of Development Associates. He had been doing that, when he could, off and on, for two weeks. Brian Kelly had done it when he could, off and on, for two weeks. They had learned that Alan Garner arrived every morning by nine. That Gino and Vinnie showed up when they felt like it. And that nobody else showed up at all.

It was hot. The windows were open. There was no breeze. The city smelled hot. Close hot. City hot. Hot asphalt. Hot metal. Hot brick. Hot exhaust. Hot people. The Explorer had air-conditioning. But a car parked all day with its motor running would, after a time, attract attention. Jesse had learned a long time ago how to sit almost motionless for as long as he needed. He'd learned how to relax his shoulders and widen his mind, and breathe easily, and sit.

As he sat, Brian Kelly came to the car and got in beside him.

'Gino come out and confess yet?' Kelly said.

'Surprisingly, no,' Jesse said.

'Well, maybe I got something for you,' Kelly said. 'I called your office and they said you were here.'

'I'm here a lot,' Jesse said.

'That nun,' Kelly said. 'Sister Mary John. She wants to talk with you. But she forgot what police department you worked for.'

'And called you?'

'No. She called Bobby Doyle. He called me. Didn't you leave a card?'

'She must have lost it.'

'Well,' Kelly said. 'She's probably thinking of salvation and all that.'

Jesse nodded.

'She say what she wanted?'

'No. Just that she wants to see you.'

Jesse looked at his watch.

'Been here all morning?' Kelly said.

'Since quarter to nine,' Jesse said.

'And the pretty boy comes at nine. And unlocks the place.'

'That's right.'

'Gino and Vinnie show up yet?'

'Not this morning,' Jesse said.

'They must be developing something off-site.'

'For all I've seen,' Jesse said, 'they haven't ever developed anything on-site. Nobody but the pretty boy and Gino and Vinnie ever come here.'

'That's the evidence I've developed,' Kelly said.

'If there's something going on with young girls, it doesn't seem to be going on here.'

'Not while we're looking,' Kelly said.

'Which, between us, is most of the time.'

'But not all,' Kelly said.

'No.'

They were silent. The heat pressed on them. The street was nearly empty. The metal exterior of the car was too hot to touch.

'You're putting a lot of time on this,' Kelly said.

Jesse nodded.

A single yellow cab rolled by, going slowly, as if it were too hot to drive fast.

'I worked homicide for a while,' Kelly said. 'I always hated it when it was a kid.'

'Yes.'

They were quiet again. Kelly shrugged.

'Not every case gets solved,' Kelly said. 'You worked homicide for a while. You know that.'

'I do,' Jesse said.

They were quiet again.

'I'm up the street,' Kelly said after a while. 'You want to go see that nun, I can sit here and do nothing for a while.'

'That would be good,' Jesse said.

'You find out anything interesting, you'll let me know.'

'I will,' Jesse said.

38

The basement room was cool. There was an air conditioner in the window near the ceiling. Sister Mary John was wearing cutoff jeans and a tank top.

When Jesse came in, he said, 'Jesse Stone.'

'I remember,' Sister said.

'You have something helpful? About Billie Bishop?'

'I don't know. Most of the girls that we have here come and go without a trace. We have a first name, or a nickname, and no last name, and no address. They are not required to tell us any more about themselves than they wish to. Our rules are simple. No drugs. No alcohol. No sex partners.'

'Sex partners?'

Sister smiled.

'Some years ago one of the girls was using the shelter as a place to ply her trade. We cannot allow a bordello to operate under our auspices, so we added a "no men" rule.'

'And things changed, so in the interests of sexual equality …' Jesse said.

'You understand,' Sister said.

'I do. We now call our people police officers.'

'It is good to be current,' Sister said.

'It is,' Jesse said. 'Billie Bishop?'

'Some of the girls, like Billie, when they depart, leave us a phone number or forwarding address. It occurred to me that if I went through our file of those, I might find a pattern.'

Sister paused. Jesse waited.

'And I believe I have,' Sister said.

'Sister, social worker, counselor, sleuth,' Jesse said.

'A renaissance nun,' Sister said. 'There were, in the past five years, fifteen girls who left us a phone number or address. There was no correlation among the addresses, but in the last year two of them left the same phone number.'

'Did they leave here at the same time?' Jesse said.

'No. They left about six months apart.'

'Did they overlap?'

'You mean were they here at the same time? No.'

'Did you call the number?'

'I did.'

'And?'

'It is no longer in service.'

'But you have written it down for me.'

'Yes.'

106

Sister handed Jesse a piece of blue-lined notepaper with a phone number written on it in a very smooth and graceful hand.

'In this area code?' Jesse said.

'Yes.'

Jesse took the notepaper and folded it and tucked it into his right hip pocket.

'Can you find out who had that number?' Sister said.

'Yes.'

'Do you think it will be helpful?'

'We'll see,' Jesse said. 'Do you have anything else?'

'No. I'm sorry.'

'No need to be sorry, Sister. You do good work.'

'God's work,' she said.

It was odd to hear her talk that way, Jesse thought. Even though he called her Sister, he didn't think of her, in her tank top and shorts and ornate Nike running shoes, as religious.

'He's lucky to have you,' Jesse said.

39

Across the table, through the candle flicker, Jenn's face looked like no other. Objectively, Jesse knew there were other women as good-looking as Jenn. But that was, at best, a factual conceit. At the center of his self, Jesse knew that she was the most beautiful woman in existence.

'You don't see that Abby person anymore, do you?' Jenn said.

She was wearing a short red-and-blue flowered dress with thin shoulder straps. When he had arrived at her condo, Jesse had noticed the amount of leg showing between the hem of the dress and the top of her high black boots.

'No,' Jesse said. 'Not socially.'

'How about Marcy Campbell?'

On the table between them was a bottle of Riesling, a bottle of Merlot and a bottle of sparkling water. Jesse poured her some Riesling and himself some sparkling water.

'I see Marcy sometimes,' Jesse said. 'We're friends.'

'Sex?' Jenn said.

'Do I ask you about your sex life?'

'Yes,' Jenn said. 'You do.'

'And do you tell me about it?' Jesse said.

'I admit to one.'

'Me, too,' Jesse said.

The table was set with linen napkins and good china. Jenn always liked a nice table. On a board between them she had set out an assortment of cheeses. There was French bread on a cutting board. There were apples and black grapes in a bowl.

'You don't want to walk into the sunset with Marcy,' Jenn said.

'No. We're friends. We sleep together sometimes. Neither of us wants to marry the other one.'

'She came to see me after Stiles Island,' Jenn said. 'We talked about you.'

Jesse sliced some bread, took a piece, and ate it with some blue cheese. He sipped some sparkling water. With the good bread and the strong cheese, the sparkling water tasted thin.

'She likes you,' Jenn said. 'She wondered what the future was for you and me.'

'What did you tell her?' Jesse said.

'That I didn't know.'

'At least you're consistent,' Jesse said.

'Anyone else in your life?' Jenn said.

'Woman who's a school principal in Swampscott.'

'And of course you're sleeping with her, too.'

Jesse nodded.

He felt the hot feeling he always felt with Jenn when they talked about sex: anger, and desperation, and excitement, and confusion. About her, about himself.

'I like her,' he said.

'Because you can fuck her?' Jenn said.

'No. The other way,' Jesse said. 'I can fuck her because I like her.'

Jenn turned her wineglass by the stem. Jesse drank some more sparkling water. He hated the insufficiency of the water. It was like breathing at a high altitude.

'And you like her why?'

'She's smart,' Jesse said. 'She's good-looking, she seems nice, and she likes baseball.'

'You know I date,' Jenn said.

'Yes.'

'I often sleep with my dates,' Jenn said.

'I know,' Jesse said.

Jenn stopped twirling her wineglass and drank from it.

'And still,' Jenn said. 'Here we are.'

'And where is that?'

'Between a rock and a hard place,' Jenn said. 'I can't be with you and I can't give you up.'

Jesse got up and went to the cupboard in Jenn's kitchen and found a bottle of Dewar's scotch. He put a lot of ice in a big glass, and poured a lot of the Dewar's over it. He brought the glass back to the table.

'So much for sparkling water,' Jenn said.

'So much.'

Jesse took a large swallow. He could feel it spread through him. His breathing seemed deeper. He could handle this.

'I meet men I like,' Jenn said. 'I find them attractive. I think I could, if not marry them, maybe, at least live with them. And I can't.'

Jesse took another drink. Usually he had it with soda.

'Because?'

'On the surface it's because they turn out to be badly flawed. Drink too much, or selfish, or womanizers, or dishonest, or emotional cripples or people for whom sex is entirely about them … something. And I have to break up with them.'

Jesse waited.

'My shrink says maybe their flaws are their appeal.'

Jesse was quiet. Jenn finished the wine in her glass and Jesse poured her some more.

'He says maybe I find this kind of man because it's what I deserve for leaving you,' Jenn said. 'And maybe it ensures that I won't marry them and leave you for good.'

The scotch was working. The hard weight in his center was less.

'And all this is unconscious?' Jesse said.

'Mostly,' Jenn said. 'But it's right. I know it is. It resonates the way something does when it's right.'

'So you don't want to leave me for good.'

'I can't,' Jenn said. 'I can't even think about a life without you in it.'

'But you don't want to be my wife again.'

'I don't know. God Jesus, don't you think if I knew what to do I would do it? Sometimes I get so scared of losing you I can't breathe.'

'And when you think about coming back?' Jesse said.

'I get so scared I can't breathe,' Jenn said.

Jesse drank the rest of his scotch. He got up and went to the kitchen and got more ice and more scotch and brought it back to the table. He sat across from her with the candlelight moving softly between them. Jenn put her hand out on the tabletop toward him.

'I'll get better,' Jenn said. 'I'm doing good in therapy. I'll get better.'

Jesse put his hand on top of hers.

'Well,' he said, 'I think my best bet is to hang around and see how it comes out.'

Jenn started to cry gently. Jesse patted her hand. He knew how she felt.

40

Jesse had a lunch scheduled with Norman Shaw on Paradise Neck at the Boat Club. He arrived a few minutes late and found Shaw at the bar, talking with someone.

'Chief Stone,' Shaw said. 'Michael Wasserman.'

Jesse shook the man's hand.

'Wasserman's organizing an event,' Shaw said. 'And I'm agreeing to be honorary chair.'

Jesse nodded.

'I'll get a table,' Jesse said. 'You can join me when you're through.'

'I always sit at the same table,' Shaw said. 'Just tell the girl you're joining me.'

The table was at the window, and from it, Jesse could see the town proper, rising up from its working waterfront, to the town hall bell tower at the top of the hill. He watched Shaw shake hands again with Michael Wasserman and come across the room toward him. Shaw had on cream-colored slacks and a raspberry-colored linen jacket over a forest green polo shirt.

'Great view, isn't it?' he said as he sat down.

'Yes.'

A gray-haired motherly looking waitress appeared immediately.

'Want a drink?' Shaw said.

'Iced tea,' Jesse said.

Shaw made a face as if the thought of iced tea were repellent.

'Ketel One on the rocks,' he said without looking at the waitress. 'Twist.'

'Thank you, Mr. Shaw,' the waitress said, and plodded away.

Shaw picked up a menu.

'Food's mediocre here,' he said. 'But the view's great and they mix you a hell of a cocktail.'

Jesse thought about the mixing skill involved in putting together a vodka on the rocks. What Shaw meant is what most drinkers meant. The drinks were large.

The waitress brought their drinks, took their lunch order, and left them alone. The vodka was in a wide lowball glass. Shaw took a long pull on it, the way people drink beer.

'So, Stone,' Shaw said, leaning back in his chair. 'What can I do for you?'

As he spoke he didn't look at Jesse. He looked around the room.

'I'm interested in your relationship with Gino Fish.'

Shaw continued to scan the room. 'Why?' he said.

'His name came up in a case,' Jesse said.

'What case?'

'Have you spent much time with Gino?' Jesse said.

'What's this about? You talked with my wife, didn't you? Gino's a casual friend.'

Shaw spotted someone on the other side of the dining room, and smiled, and nodded and with his forefinger made a little jabbing gesture of recognition.

'Michael DeSisto,' Shaw said. 'Runs some kind of school out in Stockbridge.'

'When did you see Gino last?' Jesse said.

Shaw nodded at someone else, near the bar. He shrugged in answer to Jesse's question.

'I see a lot of people,' Shaw said. 'Hard to keep track.'

'I always thought writers were alone a lot,' Jesse said.

He had in fact never thought that, but he needed to keep Shaw talking. Jesse was pretty sure that Shaw would not stop with one vodka.

'When I write, I write,' Shaw said. 'When I party, I party. What is it you're after, Stone?'

Jesse smiled his friendliest smile, but it didn't help anything, because Shaw wasn't looking at him. He was still looking around the dining room. Jesse wondered if he was desperate to be recognized, or if maybe it was a posture, designed to show Jesse how little importance Shaw attached to him.

'No idea,' Jesse said. 'I'm hoping I'll know it when I see it.'

Shaw nodded without paying much attention and gestured at the waitress. Without further instructions she brought him another vodka. Jesse smiled to himself. Boozers were predictable, Jesse thought, and don't I know it. When the drink came, Shaw picked it up and stood.

'Excuse me a minute,' he said. 'Got to say hello to an old friend.'

Standing, he took a swallow of the vodka and then carried the glass with him to a table of four well-groomed women having lunch. He stood with a hand on the back of a chair, bending over the table, holding his drink in the other hand. He said something. The women laughed. Jesse waited. Shaw had as much swagger, Jesse thought, as a guy with a potbelly, skinny legs, and a silly haircut could achieve. The women laughed again. Shaw laughed with them. Then he kissed one of them on her perfect blond head and came back to Jesse's table. As he walked past the waitress, he murmured to her. Shaw sat back down across from Jesse and looked out at the harbor.

'I've fucked all four of those broads at one time or another,' Shaw said.

'Isn't that nice for you?' Jesse said. 'When's the last time you saw Gino Fish?'

The waitress appeared with a new vodka for Shaw. It was a double. Shaw took a large swallow.

Shaw leaned back in his chair again and seemed somehow to expand. For the first time since they had been seated, Shaw looked straight at Jesse.

'Actually, Gino and I are talking about doing a book together.'

Under the pink-toned sun color on his face, the broken blood vessels made a darker red web on the skin above his cheekbones.

Jesse said, 'Un-huh.'

'About the gangster life,' Shaw said. 'Disaffection, opposition, freedom, violence.'

'Un-huh.'

Shaw drank some more.

'This country started in rebellion against established laws,' Shaw said.

Jesse nodded.

'And Gino Fish, in himself, is almost entirely outside any established norms.'

'Un-huh.'

Shaw grinned suddenly, almost genuinely, at Jesse.

'Sort of a queer *Godfather*,' he said.

'How do you collaborate?'

'Gino and I get together, couple times a week,' Shaw said.

Despite the fact that he was clearly drunk, Shaw was focused as he talked about his writing, in a way he had not been before that.

'And talk?'

'Yeah. Gino likes to talk about himself.'

Lunch arrived.

'When the book gets written,' Jesse said, 'do you share the royalties?'

'Everybody thinks it's royalties,' Shaw said. 'It ain't. It's the advance, stupid. You know?'

Jesse ate some clam chowder. Shaw paid no attention to his scrod. His speech had thickened noticeably. He'd been at the bar when Jesse arrived. He'd had three, one of them a double, since Jesse had arrived. The conversation wasn't going to last too much longer.

'So he gets half the advance?'

'Naw, it's all mine,' Shaw said. 'Gino jus' wants a book about him. He …'

Shaw stopped talking for a moment and looked at Jesse as if he were having trouble remembering who Jesse was. Then he put his head down and rested it on top of his scrod and went to sleep.

41

Suitcase Simpson came into Jesse's office trying not to look self-important.

'Got the info from the phone company,' he said to Jesse. 'That phone number used to belong to a guy named Alan Garner. No longer in service.'

'Got an address?'

'Yeah. In Brighton, but he moved last year.'

'I know where he is,' Jesse said.

Simpson stared at him.

'How you know that?' he said.

'I'm chief of police,' Jesse said.

'Oh,' Simpson said. 'Yeah. I forgot. You going to talk with this guy?'

Jesse shook his head.

'We'll watch him,' Jesse said.

'We?'

'You ever do any surveillance?'

'Jesse. I'm a cop in Paradise, Mass.,' Simpson said. 'What the hell am I going to surveil?'

'Go put on some civvies,' Jesse said. 'Time you learned.'

Driving into Boston from the north, there was a choice between the tunnel under the harbor and the bridge over the Mystic River. The tunnel was a little shorter, from Paradise, but on the Boston end you came up out of the tunnel into the boiling confusion of the largest urban renewal project in the country. Jesse took the bridge.

As they arched down toward the Charlestown end they could look down at the merge of the river and the gray sprawl of the harbor to their left. Below them was the old Charlestown Navy Yard, now mostly condominiums. Straight ahead the individuated buildings coalesced into skyline.

Tremont Street was so hot that the asphalt was soft. They parked on a hydrant and Simpson got out and bought a cup of coffee and a large Coke at a convenience store while Jesse stayed in the car looking at Development Associates of Boston. When he got in the car, he handed Jesse the Coke.

'My mother always used to tell me to drink hot stuff in hot weather,' Simpson said. 'Because being hot inside would make you feel cooler outside.'

Jesse was silent.

'You think that makes any sense?' Simpson said.

'Sure.'

'You think it's true?'

'No.'

Simpson nodded and settled back with his coffee. Jesse knew he still half believed it. He was only about ten years older than Suitcase, but he felt like his father.

'Who we looking at here?' Simpson said.

'Alan Garner works for Gino Fish. Gino Fish is the guy whose phone number Billie Bishop left when she departed the shelter.'

Simpson was sweating. His face was red. Jesse could see him thinking.

'And two other girls left his phone number at the same shelter,' he said.

Jesse nodded. Suit wasn't stupid, but his mind had to move slowly over the surface of information before he possessed it. Jesse gave him time.

After a time Simpson said, 'Well, that would be a really big coincidence.'

'Really big,' Jesse said.

'So why not go in and confront him with it?'

'And he says, I don't know anything about it, and what do we say?'

Suitcase drank some more coffee.

'I think it works,' he said.

'Drinking hot stuff?'

'Yeah.'

'Your mother tell you to run cold water over the inside of

your wrist to cool your blood?'

Simpson was surprised.

'Yeah.'

Jesse smiled.

'We could try to find those other girls,' Simpson said. 'See what they could tell us.'

'One's named Mary,' Jesse said. 'The other one is Jane. Or so they told Sister.'

'No last names?'

'Nope.'

'You know where they came from, we could check Missing Persons …'

'I don't know where they came from. I doubt that the names are real.'

'But they left a real phone number.'

'Kids need to hang on to something,' Jesse said.

'I don't know what you mean.'

'However fucked up,' Jesse said, 'kids don't want to just disappear.'

'They need to feel connected?'

'To something,' Jesse said.

Simpson took another sip of coffee. The sweat ran down his face in front of each ear.

'Careful,' Jesse said. 'You don't want to get a chill.'

'I don't know what we're looking for here,' Simpson said.

'Me, either,' Jesse said.

'So how we going to know when we see it?'

Jesse smiled.

'It's a chief of police thing,' Jesse said.

42

Today they were in Simpson's Dodge pickup, parked farther down Tremont Street, watching Development Associates of Boston in the rearview mirror. Jesse went to use the washroom at the Boston Ballet building, showing his badge in the lobby to forestall discussion.

'First rule of stakeout,' Jesse said when he came back. 'Locate near a place you can take a leak.'

'We going to follow somebody if they leave? Gino, or the receptionist guy?'

'Nope.'

'So why are we here?'

'See what happens.'

'Why don't we follow them?'

'I don't want to spook them,' Jesse said.

'You think they'd spot us?'

'People like Gino need to be pretty alert,' Jesse said. 'If somebody's alert, it's pretty hard to tail them alone.'

'So we're just going to sit here forever?'

'In another couple days,' Jesse said, 'we'll double-team them.'

'Use two cars?'

'Yes.'

'You and me in two cars?'

'Yes.'

'So this is sort of like training.'

'Sort of,' Jesse said.

'That'll be so cool,' Simpson said.

Jesse nodded.

Across the street, Vinnie Morris came up the stairs in front of the office and out onto Tremont.

'That the receptionist?' Simpson said.

Jesse smiled. 'That's the shooter,' he said. 'Vinnie Morris.'

'Doesn't look like anything special,' Simpson said.

'He's supposed to be very good,' Jesse said. 'Look at me and we'll pretend to be talking.'

'Look at you?'

'Yes. Nod your head. I'm saying something really important which is why we're sitting here in the parked car. You understand?'

Suitcase was looking at Jesse, nodding his head vigorously.

'You think he'd get wise seeing us sitting here?'

'He might,' Jesse said. 'Guys like him and Gino are very careful.'

'That why we're using my car today?' Simpson said. 'So they won't see the same one twice in a row?'

'That's right,' Jesse said.

Simpson continued to nod overtly. Jesse grinned.

'And don't overact,' he said.

In the outside mirror Jesse watched Vinnie Morris move up the street toward the sandwich shop where Simpson had bought them coffee when they'd arrived. In a few minutes he came back carrying coffee in a tall paper cup.

'Think he's been talking to your mother?' Jesse said.

'Nobody talks to my mom,' Simpson said. 'They listen.'

Vinnie Morris went back down the stairs into the office again. The truck windows were open. There was no breeze. Jesse could smell the hot smell of the sidewalk. In the middle of the afternoon, Brian Kelly came by and tapped on the side window.

'It's okay,' Jesse said. 'He's a cop.'

Kelly squeezed into the front seat of the truck beside Simpson.

Jesse introduced them.

'You got anything?' Jesse said to Kelly.

'Nope, I was going to ask you the same thing.'

'We got two more shelter girls left a forwarding number. This time Alan Garner.'

'Who's he?'

'Gino's receptionist.'

'And main squeeze?'

'I don't know, does Gino usually squeeze his receptionists?'

'Usually part of the job description,' Kelly said. 'Or so they tell me at OCU.'

'You mean these guys are gay?' Simpson said.

'I'm guessing about Garner,' Kelly said. 'But Gino's pretty certain.'

'I want to put Garner and Gino under surveillance. You got anybody you can spare?'

'I look like the CO?' Kelly said. 'I can spare me. On my own time.'

'How come you need more guys, Jesse?'

'You need a couple on Garner and a couple on Gino,' Jesse said. 'What about Vinnie?' he said to Kelly.

Kelly shook his head.

'Vinnie does what he does,' Kelly said. 'For hire. You're looking for a missing kid, or something like that, Vinnie isn't going to do you any good.'

'Why not?' Simpson said.

Jesse smiled.

'Vinnie doesn't fuck with kids,' Kelly said.

'A shooter with standards?' Simpson said.

'Whatever,' Kelly said.

'So there's you and me,' Jesse said to Kelly.

'When I'm not wasting my time working, or sleeping, or trying to get laid,' Kelly said.

'And Suit is three,' Jesse said.

'How many we need?' Simpson said.

'We could get by with three more,' Jesse said. 'Five more would be perfect.'

'Why so many?' Simpson said.

'Two cars so we can bracket Gino. Two for the receptionist.'

'So that's four,' Simpson said.

'What happens if one of them gets out of the car and starts walking?' Jesse said.

Simpson nodded.

'Can you spare anybody else?' Kelly said to Jesse.

'I only got ten cops left,' Jesse said.

'Maybe I can get Bobby Doyle interested,' Kelly said. 'Otherwise we're it, and part of the time it's just you.'

'Part of the time it's probably not any of us,' Jesse said. 'Once in a while we need to lead our lives.'

Kelly looked surprised.

'You do?' he said.

43

'You drink more when you're sad?' Dix said.

'No,' Jesse said. 'I think it's more when I'm happy.'

'You drink more when you're with her?' Dix said.

'I did this time,' Jesse said.

'Because you were happy?'

'No,' Jesse said. 'I wasn't happy.'

'Scared?'

'No.'

'What?'

'I don't know exactly,' Jesse said. 'We were talking about being with other people.'

'You talk about this before?'

'Yes.'

'You always get drunk?'

'I don't remember,' Jesse said.

'How do you feel when you think of her with another man?'

Jesse shook his head.

'Exciting?' Dix said.

'Jesus Christ!' Jesse said.

Dix waited.

'I'm not that sick,' Jesse said.

Dix remained blank. Jesse was silent for a time.

'I don't know why,' he said.

Dix almost smiled.

'What?' Jesse said.

Dix didn't answer.

'It's not about sex,' Jesse said.

'Sure it is,' Dix said. 'It's always about sex.'

'It's about other things, too,' Jesse said.

He felt as if he were retreating slowly, giving up one position after another, modifying as he went.

'It is always about other things, too,' Dix said.

'So why *do* I want to know?' Jesse said.

Dix smiled and didn't say anything.

'For crissake,' Jesse said. 'Is this a fucking game where you know and I try to guess?'

'Knowledge is power,' Dix said.

'Power to do what?' Jesse said.

'Participate,' Dix said.

Jesse thought about the surge of fear and anger and desire that filled him almost to overflowing when he thought of her with another man. He knew that the passion, the nearly voyeuristic need to know, had nothing to do with curiosity, and, he realized, nothing to do with disapproval. Dix was right. The penetrating need to be privy was a kind of participation. Not just in the act, but in her life. Not knowing was exclusion. The idea startled him.

'So it's not just him and her,' Jesse said. 'It's him, her and me.'

'Better than nothing,' Dix said.

'I hate thinking about her with another man.'

Dix nodded.

'And I hate to be excluded,' Jesse said.

Dix nodded again. The two of them sat there in silence.

'A rock and a hard place,' Jesse said.

Dix smiled.

'Enough to drive a man to drink,' he said.

44

'Kelly ever get that guy Bobby Doyle to help us out on surveillance?' Simpson asked.

Jesse shook his head.

'Doyle's got a wife and five kids, Kelly told me. Says he wastes his free time with them.'

Simpson shook his head.

'I hate when that happens,' he said.

Jesse smiled. Across the street and down from where they were parked, Gino's black Lexus pulled in at the curb. Gino Fish and Vinnie Morris came up the stairs from the office and got in. The car pulled away down Tremont.

Simpson looked at Jesse.

'Aren't we going after them?'

'No.'

'We're not?' Simpson said. 'What the hell are we sitting here in the heat for?'

'Alan Garner hasn't come out.'

'So?'

'It's why we need more people,' Jesse said. 'We can either follow Gino or stay with Alan.'

'We haven't had a lot of luck following Gino,' Simpson said.

Jesse nodded.

'Pretty Boy comes out and walks, I'll take him on foot,' Jesse said. 'You trail in the car, but not close. You lose us, come back here.'

They exchanged places so that Simpson was at the wheel. Suit was wearing a bright, flowered, short-sleeved shirt, the tails of which hung outside his jeans and covered the service pistol on his belt. Jesse wore a white tee shirt. He had a short gun in an ankle holster. Traffic went by with windows up and air-conditioning on high. Ahead of them, three guys in tank tops and yellow helmets, protected by a folding yellow barrier, were in and out of a manhole.

'I wonder if it's cooler underground,' Simpson said.

'Cellars are usually cooler,' Jesse said.

Alan Garner came up the steps from the Development Associates office and began to walk toward them on the other side of the street.

'Here we go,' Jesse said.

Garner continued past them. When he was far enough past, Jesse got out.

'Don't U-turn right here,' Jesse said. 'Sit for a couple

minutes, then go down a ways.'

Simpson nodded and Jesse began to walk up his side of the street in the same direction that Garner was walking on the other side. Garner walked as if he weren't going anyplace. In fifteen minutes they were at the south corner of Boston Common where Boylston crosses Tremont, near the old cemetery. Garner crossed Boylston Street with the light and waited patiently for the walk signal. Jesse was too close behind him. He paused and looked down Boylston Street uncertainly for a moment and let Garner get farther ahead. Garner had seen him once, in Gino's office. He tilted the blue L.A. Dodgers hat farther forward over his eyes and put both hands in his pockets. Tremont Street was one-way now, he knew Suit would have to go around. Jesse smiled. *I hope he doesn't get lost.*

They walked up Tremont Street across from the Common where a lot of people carrying backpacks, wearing shorts and sunglasses, were looking at maps. One of them was taking a picture of a fat woman standing so that the McDonald's across the street would serve as a background. Garner went into the McDonald's and came out in a moment carrying a large diet Coke in a big paper cup with a clear plastic lid. There was a straw stuck through the little hole in the lid, and Garner took a thoughtful pull on the diet Coke as he walked.

At the corner of Tremont and Park, where the entrance to the Park Street subway station spread out into a kind of plaza, Garner crossed. There was a newspaper vendor on the plaza and somebody selling souvenirs from a pushcart, and somebody else selling popcorn. Kids with lavender hair and nose rings lingered on the corner. Jesse lingered on the far side of Tremont, waiting to see which way Garner would go. If he turned in to the subway entrance, Jesse could sprint if he needed to, without Garner seeing him. Garner went and sat on a wooden bench at the edge of the plaza, across from the Park Street Church. Jesse walked a block past Park Street, up Tremont, and crossed and went back down and stopped in front of the church to read the historical plaque out front. Garner was to Jesse's left across Park Street. An adolescent girl came and sat on the bench beside him. She had on cowboy boots over black spandex tights. An oversized white tee shirt hung to her thighs. A small black purse hung on a gold chain from her shoulder. Her lipstick was black. Her face was pale. She had a great deal of shoulder-length black hair. Garner patted her thigh. The girl said something to him and giggled. He offered her a sip of his diet Coke and she took a long pull on the straw.

Jesse saw his Explorer coming down Park Street toward him. *Way to go, Suit*, Jesse said to himself. He didn't look at the car. It turned onto Tremont and moved on.

The girl took a pack of Virginia Slims out of her purse and got out a cigarette. Garner lit it for her. She took in a long drag and then let the smoke out slowly through her nostrils. Garner took an envelope from the inside pocket of his silk tweed jacket and handed it to the girl. She giggled again. *About the same age as Billie Bishop.* Garner got up and patted the girl on the head and started back down Tremont Street. The girl sat for a minute looking at the envelope, then stood and started down across the Common. *The lady or the tiger?* Jesse thought. *I can always find Garner again.* He set off across the Common after the girl.

The girl was easy to follow. She paid no attention to anyone around her as she walked diagonally across the Common and crossed at Charles Street into the Public Gardens. She walked as if she were listening to something and walking to its beat. They crossed the miniature bridge over the swan boat pond and past the statue of Washington. The girl paused, dropped her cigarette butt into the water, took out another one, lit it, and walked on. As they walked up Commonwealth Avenue along the mall, Jesse took off his sunglasses and turned his Dodgers cap around so that he wouldn't look quite the same if she happened to look back.

At Exeter Street the girl paused, took out her envelope and

looked at it again. Then she turned into a brownstone building. Jesse was close now. He saw her press the top button of a row beside the front door. She waited for a moment, then opened the door and walked in. The door swung shut behind her. Jesse crossed the street, read the name on the top bell and copied it down. T. P. Pollinger. Then he went back to the mall and sat on a bench and waited.

In an hour and twenty minutes the girl came out, looking just as she had when she went in. He followed her back down Commonwealth, his hat now stuffed in his back pocket, his sunglasses back on. She turned up Dartmouth Street. Crossed Boylston to Copley Square. Crossed the square to the Copley Plaza Hotel, got in a cab and drove away.

Jesse stood on St. James Avenue outside the hotel and watched as the cab disappeared up Huntington Avenue.

Well, he thought, *I've still got T. P. Pollinger.*

45

'How are you doing with Dix?' Jenn said.

'He's tough,' Jesse said.

They were walking on Newbury Street. It was Saturday and the street was crowded with thirtyish men and women dressed in high-styled weekend casual clothes.

'He's in a tough business,' Jenn said.

She stopped to look at some shoes in a store window.

'I love those shoes,' Jenn said.

'So why don't you buy them?' Jesse said.

'Because I haven't looked enough,' Jenn said. 'I might see something down the street that I like better.'

They moved on.

'Do you like him?' Jenn said.

'Dix? He's hard.'

'So are you,' Jenn said.

'Glad you noticed.'

'Not like that,' Jenn said. 'You are like a cold stone when you need to be.'

'So?'

'So you are not hard with me, or with people who don't require it.'

'Yeah?'

'So maybe that's how it is with Dix. I mean, how hard can he be if he chooses to do what he does?' Jenn said.

'True,' Jesse said.

'Is he doing you any good?' Jenn said.

'Yeah, I think he is.'

'Can you say?'

'Not yet,' Jesse said. 'We're ranging pretty far afield.'

'Are you talking about us?' Jenn said.

'Yes.'

Jenn paused to look at a pantsuit on a mannequin in another window.

'That's adorable,' Jenn said.

'Don't you have one just like it?'

'No. I used to have one that color. But I've never owned one with that cut.'

'Of course not,' Jesse said.

'Is there a connection between me and your drinking?' Jenn said.

'I drank too much before I met you,' Jesse said.

'Do you see him regularly?' Jenn said.

'Twice a week if I can,' Jesse said. 'Sometimes I can't.'

'Will you stay with it?'

'Yes.'

Jenn patted him lightly on the back.

'You?' Jesse said.

'Stay in therapy?'

'Yes.'

'Oh, God yes,' Jenn said. 'I may be a lifer.'

Jenn stopped suddenly and looked across the street.

'Come on,' she said and slid through the motionless traffic

to a store window on the other side of Newbury. Jesse followed. Jenn was staring at a pair of jewel-studded bright blue silk shoes with a high heel and a strap and long, pointed toes.

'Those are the shoes,' she said.

And they went into the store.

46

'Maybe it was his niece,' Kelly said.

Jesse rang the bell.

'We can ask him,' Jesse said.

Over the intercom a voice said, 'This is Pollinger.'

'This is Brian Kelly. I'm with the Boston Police Department.'

'Police?'

'Yes, sir.'

'I'll come down,' Pollinger said.

The intercom fell silent. Jesse took his badge out and put it on his belt so it would show. In about a minute a man opened the door as far as the chain bolt would allow.

'There are two of you,' the man said.

Kelly showed his badge.

'Yes sir. I'm Kelly, this is Jesse Stone.'

The man looked hard at Kelly's badge.

'Could you hold it a bit closer to the door?' the man said. Kelly held it right up to the small opening. The man took a long time examining it.

'Will you need to come in?' he said.

'You T. P. Pollinger?' Kelly said.

'Yes.'

'It would be better if we came in,' Kelly said.

'Excuse me, I have to close the door to take the chain off.'

'Sure,' Kelly said.

The door closed. The chain slid back, and the door opened.

'I'm Trip Pollinger,' the man said. 'What is this about?'

He was slender and white-haired. His face was young and evenly tanned. He wore a dark brown silk tweed jacket over a light tan silk tee shirt, tan linen trousers and coffee-colored loafers and no socks. *On a Tuesday morning?* Jesse thought. *At home? I normally sit around the house in sweatpants.*

'Perhaps we shouldn't talk in the hall,' Kelly said.

'Oh, excuse me. Where are my manners?' Pollinger said. 'Please come this way.'

The room was long and narrow and brightened by a floor-to-ceiling window at the far end. There were two skylights in the ceiling. It was furnished in the kind of angular modern furniture that Jesse had seen in showroom windows, but never in a home. A Picasso hung over the sofa. It showed a man/bull having his way with a woman. Jesse assumed it was a reproduction copy. Pollinger didn't look that affluent.

'Would you like coffee?' Pollinger said. 'Something to drink? A Coke? Perrier? I assume I can't offer you anything hard while you're on duty.'

Kelly said, 'No thank you,' and nodded at Jesse.

'Mr. Pollinger,' Jesse said. 'Yesterday afternoon I followed a very young woman to your apartment and waited outside for an hour and twenty minutes until she came out. She then walked over to Copley Square and caught a cab and I lost her.'

'A young woman?'

'A girl,' Jesse said. 'Maybe fifteen.'

'You followed her?'

'Yes, sir. She rang your bell, and went in, and stayed for eighty minutes.'

'I don't know anything about it,' Pollinger said.

'I want to find that girl,' Jesse said.

'There wasn't any girl,' Pollinger said.

'She was sent by Alan Garner.'

'Did he tell you that?'

'I'm not after you, Mr. Pollinger, I'm after the girl.'

'I don't know anything about a girl,' Pollinger said.

Jesse sighed. He looked at Kelly. Kelly shrugged.

'Easy or hard,' Kelly said. 'Doesn't matter to me.'

'What do you mean?' Pollinger said.

He looked at Jesse.

'What does he mean by that?'

Jesse didn't answer for a time, letting the question hang in the quiet.

'Here's what I think,' Jesse said finally. 'I think that the girl, who is almost certainly underage, came here to have sex with you. I assume for money.'

'Could be charm,' Kelly said. 'He's very charming.'

'I don't think he's charming,' Jesse said.

Kelly shrugged. 'No accounting for taste,' he said.

'And,' Jesse said to Pollinger, 'I bet it's not the first time. And I bet if we start asking all your neighbors, and everybody where you work, if you are having paid sex with underage girls, sooner or later I bet we'll prove it.'

'No,' Pollinger said.

Kelly pulled a straight-backed chrome chair from the dining table and pushed it toward Pollinger.

'You wanna sit down?' he said.

Pollinger sat.

'I don't want you asking around about me. I haven't done anything wrong.'

'So tell us about the girl?' Jesse said.

'Maybe I should have a lawyer,' Pollinger said.

'If you think you need one,' Jesse said.

'No … I … if I tell you, will you leave me alone?'

'Sure,' Jesse said.

'I'm a financial manager,' Pollinger said. 'I have fiscal responsibility. I can't …'

'Mum's the word,' Kelly said.

'Her name's Dawn,' Pollinger said. 'I don't think she's underage.'

'And I know you would care,' Jesse said. 'What's her last name?'

'I don't know. But I have a phone number.'

'Garner's?'

'No.'

Pollinger stood and went to a sideboard and took a piece of notepaper from a drawer. He handed it to Jesse. There was a phone number written on it in black ink. The hand was childish. The zero had a smiley face.

'I don't think she was supposed to give it to me,' Pollinger said. 'She made me promise not to tell Alan.'

'Cut out the middle man,' Kelly said. 'Enterprising girl.'

'You get other girls from Alan?' Jesse said.

Pollinger nodded. He was looking hard at the texture of his subtle gray wall-to-wall carpeting.

'They all teenyboppers?' Kelly said.

'They are young women,' Pollinger said.

'I'll bet,' Kelly said.

'Ever spend time in Paradise?' Jesse said.

'I've been up there. They have a nice restaurant on the town wharf.'

Jesse nodded.

'Ever know a girl named Billie Bishop?' he said.

'There was a girl named Billie,' Pollinger said. 'Nice girl. They're not really whores.'

'Of course they're not,' Kelly said. 'Except that they fuck for money.'

Pollinger didn't look up from the carpet.

'Where were you, the beginning of July?'

'July?'

'Yeah. First week, after the Fourth?'

'I was in London. We went on a theater tour.'

'Can you prove it?'

'Yes. It was a package, Worldwide Theater Tours. They would have a record.'

'We'll check,' Kelly said.

'Why? Why does it matter?'

'Just routine inquiry,' Jesse said. 'You know any of Billie's other clients?'

'No.'

'She never mentioned any, even in passing?'

'No. She was, we were, ah, very businesslike.'

'Wham bam, thank you ma'am,' Kelly said.

'No. It wasn't like that. They are very nice girls. It's just that we only talked about … each other.'

'You romantic fool,' Kelly said.

47

'I ran into Mrs. Snyder at Stop & Shop,' Molly said.

Jesse nodded. He was rocked back in his swivel chair drinking coffee. The air-conditioning hummed quietly.

'She told me she's getting divorced.'

'Husband still beating on her?' Jesse said.

'No. That's the funny thing. She said he hadn't touched her since the time you and he talked.'

'So?'

Molly smiled.

'She didn't quite put it this way,' Molly said. 'But it sounds like all those years he was punching her around, she used to think if he'd only stop we could be happy. And then he stopped. And she found out she still didn't like him.'

'Can't win 'em all,' Jesse said.

'She might have won this one,' Molly said.

'Yeah,' Jesse said. 'Maybe she did.'

'You have anything to do with it?'

'With what?'

'With him not hitting her anymore.'

Jesse shrugged.

'You had a talk with him, didn't you,' Molly said.

Jesse smiled.

'Nothing official,' he said.

'And, let me guess,' Molly said. 'You told him if he ever touched her unkindly again you would do something really scary to him.'

'I'm the chief of police in this town, Moll. I can't go around threatening the very citizens I'm sworn to protect.'

'Of course you can't,' Molly said. 'Cop named Kelly called from Boston. Said he had an address for that phone number, if you want to go visit.'

'Good.'

'Suit still on surveillance in Boston?' Molly said.

'No.'

'Good,' Molly said. 'It's been mucking up the vacation schedules.'

'It has,' Jesse said

'This call from Kelly, is it about Billie?'

'I hope so.'

'You getting anywhere?'

'I think so.'

'We got an official suspect yet?'

'No.'

'Are we planning not to talk about it,' Molly said, 'until we know what we're talking about?'

'It's an approach I'm experimenting with,' Jesse said. 'I'm going into Boston. I'll be gone most of the day. We got any police business to talk about before I go?'

'We might want to talk about how come I mostly run the department and you get the chief's salary.'

'Sexism,' Jesse said, 'would be my guess.'

Molly smiled and left the office. Jesse finished his coffee and phoned Kelly.

'It's an address in Brighton,' Kelly said. 'I'll meet you in front of the new Star Market in the shopping center on Western Ave.'

'An hour,' Jesse said.

48

They were in Kelly's car, in front of a gray three-decker in Brighton.

'Pollinger's alibi holds up,' Kelly said. 'Tour company says he was in London when Billie got killed.'

Jesse nodded.

'What's this kid's name?' he said.

'Phone listing is D. P. Davis.'

'Dawn,' Jesse said.

'Maybe.'

The building had been painted brown a long time ago. Much of the paint had flaked away and a lot of bare gray clapboard was showing. There was no front yard. The first of the three front steps was hard against the sidewalk. The name Davis and the number 3A were written with black Magic Marker above one of the doorbells. Jesse rang it. Nothing happened.

'You're a small-town cop,' Kelly said. 'You don't know how to do it right.'

He put his thumb on the bell and kept it there. Nothing happened.

'That how it's done?' Jesse said.

'Could be no one home,' Kelly said.

'Or the bell's broken.'

'But the front door's unlocked,' Kelly said.

'Wow,' Jesse said.

'A trained professional,' Kelly said.

They went into the dank hallway and up two flights of sagging stairs. The stairwell was dark. There was a burned-out lightbulb in an old porcelain ceiling fixture at each landing. At the dark top of the stairs Jesse knocked on the door.

'It's good practice,' he said. 'How else do I learn?'

He knocked again. There was the sound of movement. Then silence. Then the door opened on its chain.

A young female voice said, 'Come back later.'

The door started to shut but Jesse put his foot in the opening.

'Dawn Davis?'

'What do you want?'

'Boston Police,' Kelly said.

He held up his badge.

'Police?'

'Yep.'

'It's too dark,' she said. 'I can't see what you're holding up.'

Kelly put the badge into the door opening.

'You got a light in there?' he said.

'I guess so.'

'Turn it on,' he said.

There was silence for a moment, and then a light went on inside the apartment. The girl was a shadow in the narrow door opening. She stared at the badge for a time.

'Whaddya want?' she said.

'We want to come in and talk with you,' Kelly said.

'About what?'

'About whether or not to kick in this door and bust you as a material witness in a homicide investigation,' Kelly said.

'I didn't kill nobody,' the girl said.

'Open the fucking door,' Jesse said.

The girl didn't answer for a moment, then she made a shadowy movement that might have been a shrug.

'Okay,' she said. 'Get your foot out so I can take the chain off.'

The shades were down. The room was dark except for a light from the bare bulb of a table lamp on the floor. A cookstove was against the back wall, and a sink. The floor was a brick-pattern linoleum, scuffed away in places to show the narrow floorboards underneath. There was a box spring and mattress with no sheets and a thick down comforter rumpled with sleep. There were clothes piled on the floor. A half-open door revealed a narrow bathroom with tile walls and an old tub.

'You ought to charge more,' Kelly said.

'For what?' the girl said.

She was a small girl, with big dark eyes that dominated her face. She was wearing jeans and a pink sweatshirt. The sleeves were too long and concealed her hands. She was barefooted and, except for a hint of bosom under the sweatshirt, looked about nine.

'Dawn,' Jesse said. 'We've talked with T. P. Pollinger.'

'Who?'

Jesse realized that she might not know who Pollinger was. Just a john, at an address. One of many.

'Money manager in the Back Bay,' Jesse said. 'I followed you there on Monday, after Alan Garner gave you the address.'

She bent down and picked up a pack of Virginia Slims, got a cigarette out of the pack, got a butane lighter out of her pocket, and lit the cigarette.

'So?'

'So we got prostitution if we want to arrest you,' Kelly said.

'So?'

Jesse looked at Kelly. They both smiled. She was a little girl alone in a run-down apartment with two men, and she was being tough. They both knew that the bravado of young kids was rooted mostly in ignorance. If they just braved it out they could get away with it. She was wrong this time, but both of them admired her a little.

'So,' Jesse said. 'We don't want to do that if you don't make us. What we want is Garner.'

She stared at both of them.

'What do you want Alan for?'

'Do you know a girl named Billie Bishop?' Jesse said.

'No. Why are you after Alan?'

'He might be involved in a homicide we're investigating,' Kelly said.

'Alan wouldn't kill anybody.'

Kelly sighed and took his handcuffs from his belt.

'Dawn Davis,' Kelly said. 'You are under arrest for

prostitution. You have the right to remain silent. Anything you say can be used against you in a court of law. You have the right to an attorney to assist you during questioning ...'

'Hey, come on,' Dawn said.

'Turn around,' Kelly said. 'Put your hands together behind your back.'

'Hey. No. Wait a minute, what do you want to know?'

'Is Alan Garner your pimp?' Jesse said.

'Well, he's not really a pimp. I mean, you know. He's nice.'

'Does he arrange for you to meet men, and does he take a portion of the money you receive for sexual favors?' Jesse said.

'Yes.'

'How'd you meet him?'

'Alan?'

'Un-huh.'

'Around,' she said.

'He pick you up?' Kelly said.

'Yes. He bought me lunch, and we talked. He was really nice.'

'Were you soliciting?'

'No.'

'Did he pick you up near the shelter?'

'Yes. It's like we were going along in the same direction and we started talking.'

'He initiate?' Kelly said

'What?'

'He start talking first?' Jesse said.

'I don't know. I guess so. I wouldn't have just started talking to some guy.'

'Unless you'd become a working girl,' Kelly said.

'I wasn't then, honest to God.'

'That start with Garner?' Jesse said.

'I guess so.'

Both men were quiet. Kelly put the cuffs back on his belt at the small of his back.

'He said, like, where did I live, and I go, like, I'm staying at the shelter. And he says did I run away. And I said, like, of course and he says he's helped a bunch of girls like me.'

She was talking to Jesse. Even though he'd sworn at her when they first came. Now he seemed much nicer than the other cop that was going to handcuff her. The other cop looked mean, like he might be laughing at her. But Jesse had kind eyes and he leaned forward, nodding gently, like he was interested in her.

'And?' Jesse said.

'He got me this place to stay.'

'You pay the rent?' Kelly said.

'No,' the girl said. 'I don't. Alan does for me. He gives me money, too.'

'He ever come on to you?'

'No. He's never been like that. He's really really nice.'

'Do they give money to you?'

'The men I meet? No, I guess they give it to Alan.'

'You like Alan?' Jesse said.

'Alan's the nicest person I've ever met,' she said.

49

'What are you going to do about that girl you found?' Lilly said.

They were sitting on Jesse's deck, over the harbor, looking across to Paradise Neck, as the evening settled, and the space above the water turned a faint translucent blue. Lilly was drinking white wine. Jesse had a Coke.

'Dawn Davis,' he said.

'Can you send her home?'

'She wouldn't tell us where she was from.'

'She'd rather be a whore than go home?'

'Yep.'

'Or go to jail?'

'Yep.'

'Is anybody looking for her?' Lilly said.

'Kelly checked Missing Persons, and if that's her real name, there's no paper on her.'

'Can't you fingerprint her?'

'Did,' Jesse said. 'There's no match on file. It doesn't identify her. It only tells us that there's no match on file.'

'Which means she hasn't been arrested before.'

'Probably,' Jesse said.

'How old do you think she is?' Lilly said.

'Fifteen, maybe.'

'You could contact youth services,' Lilly said.

'Sure,' Jesse said.

'You don't think much of them,' Lilly said.

'No.'

'You could arrest her, couldn't you? For prostitution?'

'Yep.'

'But you're not going to.'

'No.'

'A fifteen-year-old girl can't be left to her own devices,' Lilly said.

'We dropped her off at the shelter,' Jesse said. 'With Sister Mary John.'

'And if she runs away from the shelter?'

'We told her we'd arrest her.'

'But she might anyway,' Lilly said. 'She doesn't seem entirely law-abiding.'

'True.'

'What if she runs off? Can you still arrest whatsisname?'

'Garner?'

'Yes.'

'We still have Mr. Pollinger,' Jesse said. 'He's not going anywhere, and we can use him to nail Garner.'

With evening the heat had receded, and the salt breeze off the harbor made the deck comfortable. Jesse had his feet on the railing.

'Are you going to arrest Garner?' Lilly said.

'Sooner or later,' Jesse said.

'Why are you waiting?'

Lilly's glass was empty. Jesse stood and filled her glass and got himself another Coke.

'Won't that keep you awake?' Lilly said.

'Gotta drink something,' Jesse said.

He handed the wineglass to Lilly and sat down and put his feet back up on the rail. Early evening. End of day. Friday night. On the deck. The water, murmuring. A good-looking woman whom he liked, the slowly dwindling view of the neck across the black water. He should be having a drink. It was exactly the time for a drink. Exactly the situation.

'So why are you waiting to arrest Garner?'

'I'm not sure. I guess I don't want to stir things up until I know what I'm stirring.'

'It's still about Billie Bishop, isn't it?'

'Yes.'

'Do you have a theory?'

Jesse drank a little Coke. It had caffeine in it. It tasted like it should give him a pleasant jolt. There was none.

'Alan Garner is almost certainly recruiting runaway girls to prostitution. He doesn't seem like your standard street pimp. He treats them nice, doesn't come on to them, puts them up in a cheap apartment, and rents them out on a call basis. Maybe to a specialized market.'

'Men who like very young girls.'

'Yes. Alan works for a mobster named Gino Fish. Gino is an acquaintance of Norman Shaw, the novelist. Shaw lives in Paradise.'

'Do you think that Garner recruited Billie Bishop?'

'Maybe.'

'For this Fish person?'

'Yes.'

'Do you think that Gino Fish is supplying adolescent girls to Norman Shaw?' Lilly said.

'I have no idea. I've met Mrs. Shaw and she would certainly be sufficient for me.'

'You know that has nothing to do with it,' Lilly said.

'I know.'

'Do you think he might have sent Billie Bishop to Norman Shaw, which is how she ended up in Paradise?'

'In the lake,' Jesse said.

'Yes. Do you think?'

'What I think,' Jesse said, 'is that I'm not going to jostle any of them, until I've got enough to get them all.'

'Do you know who they all are?' Lilly said.

'Not yet.'

50

'I had a thought,' Jesse said to Suitcase Simpson.

'Excellent,' Simpson said.

'Wise guys don't make sergeant,' Jesse said. 'What I was thinking was that if Norman Shaw was banging kids like Billie, where would he do it?'

'His house?'

'You think Mrs. Shaw would have a problem with that?'

'Oh, yeah.'

'So if he's doing it, it must be someplace else.'

'You really think he's involved?'

'No. I really think he isn't,' Jesse said. 'But I don't know he isn't. I want to know. It's where the chain of connection stops.'

'Billie Bishop to Alan Garner to Gino Fish to Shaw,' Simpson said.

'Sort of.'

'Not much of a chain,' Simpson said.

'Everybody's a critic,' Jesse said. 'If you had a teenaged beauty you wanted to score, where would you go?'

'Not my high school,' Simpson said.

Jesse smiled.

'I guess I'd take her to a motel,' Simpson said.

Jesse nodded. 'You want to learn several things,' he said 'You want to learn if a guy named Norman Shaw has registered there, in, say, the last six months, whatever they got for records.'

'Would he use his real name?' Simpson said.

'Probably not,' Jesse said. 'So he couldn't use a credit card. Try to find who registered and paid cash.'

'Hotels keep records like that?' Simpson said.

'Some do. Some don't,' Jesse said. 'Sometimes you can be lucky. You'll get a clerk who remembers.'

'Shaw's pretty recognizable,' Simpson said. 'Even if he gave a false name and paid cash.'

'So what would you do about that?' Jesse said. 'If you were him?'

'Disguise?'

Jesse smiled.

'Ask if they remember a guy with a fake nose and glasses,' he said.

'Really?'

'Suit, I'm kidding you. Be easier if he had the girl register.'

'And if he was real careful,' Simpson said, 'he'd have her register at one of those places where you can park right in front of the door and go in your room once you got a key.'

'Maybe you should start with that kind of motel, close to Paradise, and then circle out. Get a picture of Shaw. And take one of Billie. Show both of them.'

'You're pulling me off shift again?'

'Special assignment,' Jesse said.

'Guys are getting kind of annoyed,' Simpson said, 'covering for me.'

'Un-huh.'

'We don't even know if Shaw's got anything to do with it,' Simpson said.

'That's true.'

'There's a thousand motels around here.'

'Un-huh.'

'Jeez, on those TV real-life cop shows they don't do this. They got all kinds of guys with microscopes and computers figuring shit out.'

'We're a small department,' Jesse said. 'We can't afford smart people.'

'This could be a total waste of time,' Simpson said.

'Ah,' Jesse said, 'you are beginning to understand the intricacies of police work.'

51

'You wanted to drink,' Dix said.

'Yes.'

'But you didn't.'

'No.'

'Why'd you want to?'

Jesse shrugged. It never occurred to him to ask why he wanted a drink. Wanting a drink was part of existence. It didn't have a why.

'Did you want one at 2:35 that afternoon?'

'I'm not that far gone,' Jesse said.

'I'll take that to mean no,' Dix said. 'So why did you want one at seven o'clock that evening?'

'What difference does it make?' Jesse said.

'None,' Dix said, 'to me.'

They were silent.

'It was, you know, you used to be a drinker,' Jesse said. 'It was the end of the day and the harbor was quiet, and we were sitting together on the deck, and later we'd have sex. I mean it was all ahead of us.'

'The romance of booze,' Dix said.

Jesse thought about that. 'Miller time,' he said.

'Soft light touching on crystal stemware, bright liquid, clean white shirt, shimmering gown, alto sax, here's looking at you, kid.'

'You think that makes me drink?'

'No. But it helps make you want to.'

'But I didn't give in this time.'

'No,' Dix said. 'You didn't.'

'Kind of late,' Jesse said.

Dix waited.

'Now I'm saying no,' Jesse said. 'Now that it's cost me my job and my marriage.'

'But you have a new job,' Dix said.

'Marriage is gone.'

'You think that's your fault?'

'Sure,' Jesse said. 'She couldn't be expected to stay with a drunk.'

'You don't think she should share the blame?'

'Sure,' Jesse said. 'I know. In every breakup there's fault on both sides, blah, blah.'

'But this one was all yours,' Dix said.

'Pretty much,' Jesse said.

'You don't think the fact that she was sleeping with other men might have contributed?'

Jesse didn't answer.

'Maybe you couldn't be expected to stay with an adulteress.'

'What are you saying?'

'If you take the responsibility for it, then it's in your hands.'

'If I broke it, maybe I can fix it,' Jesse said.

'And if you didn't break it, maybe you can't,' Dix said. 'And you have to face the scary fact that you can't control how this will work out.'

Jesse sat for a long time without speaking.

'So what's this got to do with me not drinking when I wanted to the other night?'

'What we're doing here,' Dix said, 'is a little like what you did when you were working homicide in L.A. There are incidents, we're not sure of how these incidents connect, but we register them, notice sequence, think about them.'

'Maybe because I don't love Lilly, I can spare some energy to control my drinking, instead of controlling myself when I'm with Jenn.'

'Maybe,' Dix said.

'And maybe I need to think about not drinking so I can stop being a drunk.'

'Instead of?'

'Instead of not drinking so I can be with Jenn.'

Dix nodded.

'Sometimes we clear a case,' Dix said.

52

'He used the girl to register,' Simpson said.

'If it was him.'

'Whoever it was,' Simpson said.

'Anybody see him?'

'No.'

'Where?'

'The Boundary Suites, on Route One.'

'The No Tell Motel,' Jesse said. 'Have Peter Perkins do a crime scene workup on the room.'

'It's a motel room,' Simpson said. 'There'll be a kajillion prints in there.'

'See what you can find,' Jesse said. 'You get a positive ID on the girl?'

'She registered as Elinor Bishop.'

'Anybody recognize her picture?'

'No.'

'Tell Perkins when he goes up there, use his own car,' Jesse said. 'No need to make the motel look bad.'

'I still think it's a waste of time, Jesse.'

'Of course it is,' Jesse said, 'that's one of the things cops do. We waste a lot of time.'

Simpson left the office. Jesse stood and went to the coffeemaker and poured himself another cup. He added a lot of sugar and brought the cup back to his desk. There was a picture of Billie Bishop taped to the corner of his desk calendar. He nodded at it.

'We're getting there,' he said.

He drank some coffee while he looked at her picture. The chances of Perkins finding anything they could use in a busy motel room a month after Billie's last visit were nearly nonexistent. Which would leave him with what he had now. He knew some facts. Billie had left Gino Fish's business phone number with the shelter. Alan Garner worked for Gino. Alan Garner pimped young runaways he picked up from the shelter. Billie was a young runaway who had stayed at the shelter. She turned up dead in Paradise. Norman Shaw lived in Paradise. Norman Shaw knew Gino Fish. Put all of that together, give it to a skilled prosecutor, who'll take it to the grand jury, and there will be no chance of an indictment. He could bust Garner and try to turn him, but the chances that Garner would testify against Gino were very slim. And it would send everybody else scurrying underground. If Shaw was in fact being supplied with very young girls, it probably would happen again. *We know that,* Jesse thought, *maybe we can turn him.* What about Joni Shaw? Could she be married to a pedophile and not know it? Did pedophiles have active adult sex lives? Joni was a lot younger than Shaw. Was she the first wife? If she wasn't, what had ended the previous marriage?

He got up and walked to the front desk where Molly was reading an issue of *Martha Stewart Living*.

'You ever read Norman Shaw's books?' Jesse said.

'Sure. I got every one,' Molly said. 'He's great.'

Jesse nodded, but not as if he believed her.

'How many are there?'

'Ten, I think. At least in paperback.'

'You got them at home?' he said.

'Sure.'

'I'll take the desk,' Jesse said. 'Go home and get them.'

'All ten?'

'Yeah.'

Molly stared at him for a moment. But she didn't say anything. Jesse was Jesse. She dog-eared *Martha Stewart*, put it down, got up, and went.

While she was gone, Jesse took a call about a missing bicycle, and a call reporting a rabid skunk and could someone come over and shoot it. Jesse took down the missing-bicycle information and left it on the desk for Molly. He called John Maguire on the radio and told him to go shoot the skunk.

'Make sure there's no bubble gum wrappers in the shotgun barrel,' he said.

'Hey,' Maguire said, 'I'm a law-enforcement professional.'

'Yes you are,' Jesse said. 'Go enforce that skunk.'

Molly came back into the police station with a plastic supermarket bag filled with paperback books. Jesse turned the desk over to her and took the books into his office. His coffee was gone. He poured some more. Added a lot of sugar. The less booze he drank, the more coffee he drank. Jittery was better than drunk. He sat down and pulled one of Shaw's books out of the grocery bag. The title *Outcast* was embossed in raised gold letters on the front cover. On the back cover was a picture of Norman Shaw. He looked a lot younger in the picture than he had with his forehead resting on his grilled scrod the last time Jesse had seen him. Jesse glanced through the text. The book was 456 pages long. Jesse wasn't sure he had read a total of 456 pages in his life. In the front of the book were three pages of quotes from newspaper reviews, all of them favorable, another page listing Shaw's other books and a dedication page. The dedication in *Outcast* was 'To Joni, who rescued me in time.' Jesse looked for a date. The book had been published the year before. Jesse looked through the front matter in the other books. The previous book was dedicated 'To Arlene: Toward the sunset – together.' The publication dates were four years apart. Three books previous had been dedicated 'To Cheryl:

Till the End of Time.' Jesse read a few pages of *Outcast*. He didn't like it. He put the books away and finished his coffee and got up and walked across the street to the Paradise Public Library.

He liked the library. It was one of those nineteenth-century brick-and-brownstone buildings that could just as easily have been a fire station or a jail. The research librarian smiled at him as he went by the desk. She didn't seem like a librarian. She had a good body. She wore tight clothes. And she always looked at him as if they were sharing a private joke.

He sat at a table and looked up Norman Shaw in *Who's Who*. He had been born in Bronxville, NY, August 26, 1945 s. Samuel G and Andrea (Vogal) L; m. Cheryl Anne Masters, June 5, 1975 (div. 1979); m. Arlene Marie Greene, April 21, 1980 (div. 1985); m. Felicia Jane Feinman, Oct. 16, 1989 (div. 1996); m. Joan Harriet Roth, May 21, 1999.

No book for Felicia? Or a dedication to his lawyer?

Jesse copied the Shaw entry and took it back with him across the street to his office. He handed the sheet to Molly.

'Do your phone magic,' he said. 'See if you can come up with one or more of the ex-wives.'

'In between times,' Molly said. 'When I'm not running the department.'

'That would be good,' Jesse said.

53

'Are you still seeing Dix?' Jenn asked.

They were on the footbridge over Storrow Drive, near the Hatch shell, walking toward the river.

'I am,' Jesse said.

'And?'

Jesse shrugged.

'And I'm talking with him.'

'Do you feel you're making progress?' Jenn said.

'I might be,' Jesse said.

'Can you tell me about it?'

'No, I don't think I can.'

'It's all right,' Jenn said. 'Therapy's a private thing.'

'I don't mind you knowing,' Jesse said. 'It's simply that I don't know how to talk about it. Something's happening in there, but I'm not sure what.'

'Do you like Dix?'

'It sort of doesn't matter,' Jesse said. 'He's a lot more than an alcohol counselor.'

'Yes,' Jenn said.

'You knew that when you sent me to him,' Jesse said.

'Yes.'

'Manipulative,' Jesse said.

'Absolutely.'

They went down off the bridge and started west on the esplanade along the river. College-aged kids were sunning themselves near the water, dogs chased Frisbees, small sailboats moved on the surface where the river widened into a basin.

'Are you talking about us?' Jenn said.

'Of course.'

'How is that going?'

Jesse shrugged.

'It seems to me sometimes that everything I know, I learned from you,' she said.

'But we're divorced and seeing other people.'

'I know,' Jenn said.

They crossed the lagoon on a small barrel-arched foot-bridge. Jesse stopped at the top of the arch and leaned his forearms on the railing. Jenn stopped beside him and leaned back.

'The other night I really wanted to drink,' Jesse said. 'And I didn't.'

'Why not?'

'I'm not sure. But I didn't. Almost always before when I felt that way, I did.'

'One robin doesn't mean it's spring,' Jenn said.

'I think you got the quote wrong,' Jesse said.

'You know what I mean.'

'Day at a time,' Jesse said.

'Easy does it,' Jenn said.

They both laughed.

'Friend of Bill's?' Jenn said.

Below the bridge on the lagoon three ducks with brown feathers slid along the water.

'Friend of Jenn,' Jesse said.

54

Felicia Feinman Shaw had remarried. Her current name was Felicia Teitler and she agreed to have tea with Jesse at the Four Seasons Hotel. Jesse wore a coat and tie, his gun well back on his hip so it wouldn't show if he unbuttoned his jacket. The hostess escorted Jesse to the table. Felicia Teitler was already there.

'I'm Jesse Stone, Mrs. Teitler.'

'Please, sit down,' she said.

Jesse sat.

'Thank you for agreeing to talk,' Jesse said.

'Actually I was rather curious,' she said, 'to see what aberration he's guilty of this time.'

The language was elegant, but the accent wasn't. *Money can buy the language*, Jesse thought, *but the accent is harder*.

'*He* being Norman Shaw?' Jesse said.

'Of course,' she said. 'What other aberrant jerk would we be here to discuss?'

'Tell me about some of his aberrations,' Jesse said.

Mrs. Teitler was looking at her menu. The waitress hovered.

'I'm going to have the full tea,' she said.

150

The waitress looked at Jesse.

Jesse said, 'I'll have that, too.'

He wasn't entirely sure what a full tea was. Mrs. Teitler put the menu down and smiled at him. She looked to be about fifty. She was very well made up, but small lines showed around her eyes and the corners of her mouth. Her hair was too blond. Her skin was too tan. But what Jesse could see of her body still looked good. Her teeth were very white. Her beige suit fit her well. On her left hand she wore an enormous diamond ring. She had a small pony of what appeared to be sherry.

'And what kind of tea for you, sir?' the waitress said.

'Are you allowed to have coffee?'

'Of course, sir.'

'I'll have some,' Jesse said.

Mrs. Teitler took a little sherry.

'So what did you wish to know about Norman Shaw?' she said.

'Whatever you can tell me,' Jesse said. 'We're just doing background.'

'He's done something,' Mrs. Teitler said. 'You wouldn't track me down and arrange to meet me, just for background.'

'You were his third wife,' Jesse said.

'Yes.'

The waitress brought Jesse a small silver pot of coffee. She poured some in his cup.

'Why did you divorce him?'

'Maybe he divorced me,' she said.

Jesse shook his head.

'We checked,' he said. 'You brought suit against him.'

'Well, aren't you thorough?'

'And got a dandy settlement,' Jesse said.

'I earned it,' she said.

'The basis for the divorce was adultery,' Jesse said.

'Whores.'

'Only?'

'He marries the good girls,' Mrs. Teitler said, 'but whores were his passion. My therapist said probably it was about ownership.'

'The more he paid for them,' Jesse said, 'the more valuable they were?'

'I think he liked them young, too.'

'Younger than you?'

'Apparently.'

Jesse smiled.

'Do you know any of the whores?' he said.

She shook her head. The waitress brought small sandwiches and assorted pastries and set them out. Tea was a bigger deal than Jesse had realized. He took a cucumber sandwich. Mrs. Teitler carefully put strawberry jam on a small scone and added a dollop of clotted cream.

'I preferred not to meet them,' she said. 'My attorney employed a private detective and he got affidavits from four of them that Norman had paid them for sex.'

She popped the little scone into her mouth and chewed. Jesse poured himself some more coffee.

'There were pictures, too,' Mrs. Teitler said. 'Norman agreed not to contest the divorce.'

'Did you see the pictures?'

'I preferred not to,' she said.

'I'm sorry,' Jesse said. 'This is, ah, indelicate but I need to ask. How was he at home, sexually?'

'Christ!' Mrs. Teitler said. 'A cop who says "indelicate." In bed Norman was, oh, adequate.'

'Any dysfunction?'

'You mean like he couldn't get it up?'

'Or odd sexual practices?'

Mrs. Teitler laughed. 'Sometimes I think they're all odd,' she said. 'But no. He was not a maiden's dream, but he was, ah, sufficient … when he was sober.'

Jesse nodded.

'Which was often?'

'Less so as time went on,' Mrs. Teitler said. 'You get any kicks out of asking these questions?'

'Depends on the answers,' Jesse said. 'Can you give me the name of the private detective you hired?'

'My attorney hired him. Mark Hillenbrand on State Street. Hillenbrand and Doherty.'

Jesse wrote it down in his little notebook. He smiled at her.

'How's the second marriage?' he said.

She shook her head.

'Two-time loser,' she said. 'You like older women?'

'Sure.'

'Don't tell,' she said. 'Don't swell. Grateful as hell.'

'I've heard that,' Jesse said.

55

Dick Pettier had an office over a sandwich shop on Broad Street, across the street from a Japanese restaurant. The sign on his office door read r. j. pettier, inquiries. Jesse went in.

Pettier was tall and bony with rimless glasses.

'Mark Hillenbrand called me,' Pettier said. 'Told me you'd be coming by.'

'You did the snoop work on Norman Shaw's divorce from Felicia Feinman,' Jesse said.

Pettier smiled, his teeth gleaming.

'I like to call it discreet inquiry,' he said.

'But you did it?'

'Sure.'

'You got affidavits from several hookers,' Jesse said.

'I could have gotten them from a hundred,' Pettier said.

'How old were they?'

Pettier rocked back in his swivel chair and looked thoughtfully at Jesse.

'Pretty good question,' he said.

Jesse nodded.

'They were babies,' Pettier said. 'I can't guarantee how old, but they all looked about thirteen.'

'He have an MO?' Jesse said.

'Sure. He'd meet them in a motel, sometimes four, five nights a week. Couple times he had more than one in the same night.'

'Same motel?'

'Usually.'

'Boundary Suites,' Jesse said.

'Hey,' Pettier said, 'pretty good. Yeah. Boundary Suites right there in your neighborhood.'

'He take them there?'

Pettier shook his head.

'Nope. When he got there, with me behind him, he'd go straight to the motel room. You know Boundary Suites?'

'Yeah.'

'Well, you know it's a lovers' hideaway,' Pettier said. 'Drive up to the door of the room. Go right in. No lobby to go through. Nobody to see you.'

'You know how he set it up?' Jesse said.

'Nope. I assume by phone.'

'You know who supplied them?'

'Nope. Not my job.'

'The girls always very young?' Jesse said.

'Everyone I saw.'

'If I needed you in court, could you prove what you're saying?'

'Sure. I got photos. You want to see?'

Pettier got up and went to the gray metal file cabinet to the left of his window. He took out a folder and brought it back and put it on the front of his desk where Jesse could look through it. There were pictures of a clearly recognizable Norman Shaw and different very young women, in sexually explicit action in a motel room. Shaw looked better than he did now. His belly seemed flat and he had more hair.

'Through the window?' Jesse said.

'Yeah. There's a little hill behind the room. I'd go around there with a telephoto. He never shut the lights off.'

'Or pulled the curtains.'

'Maybe he liked people to watch,' Pettier said.

'Maybe you been doing this too long,' Jesse said.

'Maybe I'm right,' Pettier said.

'You never saw him pick up these kids?'

'Nope. Never saw him pick up anybody,' Pettier said. 'Just showed up at the motel. Stayed a couple of hours and went home. Wham, bam, thank you ma'am.'

'You never saw anybody deliver them?'

'Nope. Shaw was my job. I was behind him. The broads were already there when he arrived.'

'And you don't know anything about his habits after the divorce?'

'Nope. But I'll bet he hasn't changed,' Pettier said. 'I don't know shit about psychology. But I'd say this is a guy doing something he needs to do, you know? Has to do.'

'I'd like to copy these pictures,' Jesse said. 'I'll see that you get them back.'

'Keep 'em,' Pettier said. 'I still got the negatives.'

Jesse stood and put out his hand.

'Thanks,' he said.

Pettier shook hands without getting up.

'I don't suppose you're going to tell me why you want to know all this?' he said.

'That's right,' Jesse said. 'I'm not.'

'Not my job, anyway,' Pettier said.

56

'We still can't connect Shaw with Billie Bishop,' Jesse said.

He and Kelly were in Kelly's car parked along Day Boulevard near Carson Beach. They had coffee in paper cups. A bag of donuts was on the seat between them.

'Everything but,' Kelly said.

'But we still can't connect him specifically to Billie Bishop.'

'Or Billie Bishop with Alan Garner,' Kelly said.

'Or Shaw with Garner,' Jesse said.

'Shaw's the one,' Kelly said.

'You think?'

'Yeah. The sonovabitch jumps out at you.'

'Nice if we could prove it.'

'At least we know where to look,' Kelly said.

'What we can prove,' Jesse said, 'is that Shaw likes young hookers.'

'And that he took them to a motel on the North Shore, and Billie Bishop checked into that same hotel.'

'Can we prove that he took Billie Bishop there?' Jesse said.

'You tell me,' Kelly said.

'No.'

'And if we could prove he took her there, can we prove that he killed her?'

'No.'

They were silent. Kelly took a cinnamon donut out of the bag and shook it to get rid of the loose cinnamon.

'The only connection we've got is Garner to Shaw through Gino Fish,' Jesse said.

Kelly took a bite of the donut, leaning far forward over the steering wheel so as not to get cinnamon on himself.

'Because Billie Bishop called Gino's phone number,' he said.

'Yeah. But it might be that she called Garner at Gino's office.'

'I don't like Gino for this,' Kelly said.

'Because?'

'Not his style,' Kelly said. 'Why would Gino pimp for a fucking pedophile? Risk is big and money's small.'

'Favor for a friend?' Jesse said.

'Gino?'

'He doesn't value friendship?' Jesse said.

'He's never experienced it.'

'So you think Garner was working out of Gino's office?'

'And maybe Gino don't know nothing about it.'

'Which makes the Shaw connection kind of a problem,' Jesse said.

'Big coincidence,' Kelly said.

'You can't assume coincidence,' Jesse said.

'No you can't,' Kelly said. 'Garner could know Shaw through Gino.'

'So?'

'So we're right where we were,' Kelly said.

Jesse broke off a piece of cinnamon donut and popped it in his mouth. He chewed carefully and took a sip of coffee.

'How would Gino feel if he found out Garner was running a prostitution business out of Gino's office?'

'He would be offended,' Kelly said.

They were both silent, watching a flatbed tow truck hook up to a Dodge pickup that was parked in a tow zone. A motorcycle cop was supervising.

'You think we're next?' Jesse said.

'Traffic division's a menace,' Kelly said.

The tow truck driver squirmed under the pickup and hooked his cable on the frame. Then he stood beside his truck and worked the lever and the pickup began to winch up onto the flatbed.

'So,' Jesse said. 'If Garner found out we knew about him, and were planning to talk with Gino about it …'

Kelly smiled and said, 'Bingo!'

57

There were two blue-and-white Paradise cruisers, one pulled up onto the sidewalk, nose in, blue lights still flashing, parked in front of the Atlantic Market. Jesse parked on the street behind them and got out. Behind the car that was up on the sidewalk were Anthony DeAngelo and Eddie Cox. Cox had a shotgun.

'Hostage,' Anthony DeAngelo told him. 'I think it's Snyder and his wife. You know, the one beat her up all the time?'

'Where are they?'

'Back of the store, I think,' DeAngelo said. 'By the service counter.'

'Anybody else?'

'Some customers. Couple of store people. I don't know yet how many.'

'Anybody here from the store?'

'We got one of the cashiers,' Cox said. 'She's the one came running out hollering. Store manager's on his way.'

'Got the back covered?'

'Suit and Buddy.'

'Anybody made contact?'

'I went to the front door,' DeAngelo said. 'Guy yells at me from the back. Says he'll kill her and everybody else if I try to come in.'

'I said I was just there to help. Was there something he wanted,' Cox said.

'And?'

'He said I should get out or he'd start shooting. Then he says to the broad, "Tell him," but she don't talk. I can hear her crying.'

'What about the other people in the store?'

'I don't know. I didn't see anybody.'

'Okay,' Jesse said, 'where's the cashier?'

'In Eddie's cruiser,' DeAngelo said.

In the distance there was the sound of another siren.

'That'll be Arthur,' DeAngelo said.

'Call Molly,' Jesse said. 'She covers the station. I want everyone else down here.'

DeAngelo nodded and began to speak into the microphone clipped to his epaulet. Jesse walked to the other cruiser and got in. An adolescent girl with a lot of brown hair worn up, and braces on her teeth, was sitting in the passenger seat hugging herself.

'I want to go home,' she said.

'Anybody coming to get you?' Jesse said.

'No.'

'What's your name?'

'Kate.'

'Kate what?'

'Ryan.'

'What's your phone number, Kate?'

She gave it to him.

'But no one's home,' she said.

Jesse nodded.

'Okay,' he said. 'You got a work phone for one of your parents?'

'My father works in Boston,' she said. 'My mother sells real estate.'

She gave him both numbers.

Jesse picked up the radio and called Molly and gave her the phone numbers.

'Get a parent down here for Kate Ryan,' he said.

'I'm on it,' Molly said. 'What's happening?'

Jesse put the mike away without answering.

'They'll be here soon,' he said to Kate. 'So what happened?'

'He came in the front door and right past me.'

'Snyder?'

'I don't know his name. I never seen him before.'

'You were at the checkout?'

'Yeah and he went right past me and he took out his gun and he said he was going to kill her.'

'Mrs. Snyder?'

'Yeah. She just started working, customer service, and he said he was going to kill everybody and I run out and seen that cop, and started screaming and ...' She shrugged and spread her hands. 'What if they can't find my mother or father?'

'She's a cop,' Jesse said. 'She'll find them. What kind of gun did he have?'

'Just a gun. I don't know nothing about guns.'

'Was it a handgun or something longer like a rifle or a shotgun?'

'Hand.'

Jesse took his .38 off his belt.

'Did it look like this?' Jesse said. 'Kind of round, or was it more square?'

'It might have been more square,' she said. 'I don't know. It was a gun.'

Jesse put the gun back in its holster.

'Okay,' he said. 'Did you hear him say anything else?'

'No. I run out as soon as I saw the gun and he went past me.'

'Who was in the store besides you?'

'Mario, from the meat counter … Ray the vegetable guy … some customers … Bethany, the other cashier, was on break.'

'How many customers?'

'I don't know.'

'Ten?'

'No. Not that many.'

'Five?'

'Maybe. Can you call her and see if she got my mother and father?'

'They'll be here,' Jesse said.

Peter Perkins and John Maguire had arrived.

'Murphy and Friedman are around back with Suit and Buddy,' Perkins said. 'Molly says she can't raise Martin yet.'

'Okay. Put on the vests and start clearing people out of the adjacent stores. John, take Kate across the street and stay with her.'

Jesse got out of the car. As she walked across the street with Maguire, Kate looked back once at Jesse. He smiled at her.

'They'll be here,' he said.

DeAngelo came over with a balding red-faced man who seemed out of breath.

'This is Mr. Stevens,' DeAngelo said. 'Store manager.'

'Jesse Stone. How many ways out of the store?'

'Three.'

'Where?'

'Back door. Front door. And loading door in the cellar.'

'Where's the cellar door open?' Jesse said.

'In the back, right near the back entrance but lower.'

'Any private rooms in there?'

'My office, which is up some stairs beside the service counter.'

'Bathroom?'

'Yes, behind the stairs to my office.'

'Everything else is market space?'

'Yes.'

'Any connecting ways between your store and the ones on either side?'

'No.'

'Is there a phone near the service booth?'

'Yes, sir. Inside the counter.'

Jesse handed him a cell phone.

'Dial the number,' Jesse said.

Stevens did, and handed the phone to Jesse. Jesse waited. It rang without result. Jesse counted ten rings, then broke the connection. No need to irritate Snyder.

'There a window in the bathroom?' Jesse said.

'Yes,' Stevens said. 'Frosted glass.'

'How about in your office?'

'Yes. But it's on the second floor, remember.'

A crowd had gathered across the street.

'Peter,' Jesse said. 'Get those people out of the line of fire.'

Perkins nodded and started across the street. The air was still. The high summer sound of an insect lingered above him. It was a sound he'd heard all his life. He never knew what made it, exactly. Crickets? Grasshoppers? He dialed the store again. Again he let it ring ten times and broke the connection. He had on a light-blue linen blazer and a gray tee shirt, jeans and sneakers. His gun was on his right hip, under the blazer.

161

He stood silently for a minute, staring at the store and the police cars and the crowd and the cops in their bulletproof vests. For a moment it all looked motionless, like a frozen frame in a movie. He took in some air.

A woman in a flowered yellow dress opened the front door of the market and stepped out and ran. She ducked behind DeAngelo's cruiser and fell to her knees.

'He wants to talk to Stone,' she said. 'He says he wants Stone to come in.'

She was having trouble getting enough air in.

'He said he was going to kill us all,' she said. 'He's drunk. He has a bottle and he keeps drinking.'

Jesse crouched beside her.

'Where is he?' Jesse said.

'He put the gun right in my face,' the woman said.

She was blond, with a lot of dark eye makeup.

'Where is he standing?' Jesse said.

'In the back. He said he was going to kill everybody, himself too.'

'Where are the other hostages?'

'With him. Sitting on the floor except for one woman he hangs on to. I think it's his wife.'

'Where on the floor?'

'I don't know, just on the floor.'

'No. You do know. If I'm facing him, where are the hostages? To my right or my left?'

The woman thought for a moment.

'Right,' she said.

'How far?'

'They're all sitting against the wall under the service counter, except the wife.'

Stevens was crouched behind the squad car beside them.

'Service counter is in the right rear corner of the store,' Stevens said.

Jesse nodded.

'Tell me about the hostages,' Jesse said to the woman in the yellow dress. 'How many men? How many women?'

'Two men,' she said and paused, her breath still rasping, counting in her head. 'Four women, five if you count the wife.'

Jesse stood.

'Okay,' he said to no one in particular.

He walked to his car, and standing behind it, out of sight of the store, he rearranged his revolver on his belt. Then he got a long-barreled .22 target pistol out of the car, made sure there were bullets in the cylinder, and stuck it in his belt at the small of his back, under his jacket. Then he walked back to DeAngelo.

'I'm going in. Call Suit and tell him I'm going in. I want you all to hold still. If you hear a shot then I want all of you to come, front and back ... double time.'

DeAngelo nodded and unclipped the microphone from his epaulet. Jesse turned and walked toward the market.

58

It was a small market, the kind that delivers phone orders. There were four aisles. Jesse could see the edge of the back door at the left corner. A sign that said customer service hung from the ceiling in the right back corner. An arrow pointed straight down. The two-counter checkout was to the right of the door. The store was dead quiet.

'Snyder,' Jesse said.

'Stop right there.'

'I'm stopped,' Jesse said.

Snyder appeared at the end of the cereal aisle. His wife was in front of him. In his right hand he held what looked like a nine-millimeter handgun. *Semiautomatic, maybe a Colt. At least seven rounds, maybe twice that. Not cocked.* The gun was pressed to his wife's neck. In his other hand he had an open bottle of Chivas Regal.

'Take off your coat,' Snyder said. 'I wanna see you gotta gun.'

Mrs. Snyder's face was chalk white with deep lines. Her body was rigid. Her eyes were bulging.

'Sure I've got a gun,' Jesse said. 'I'm a cop.'

He slid the blue linen jacket off and let it fall to the floor. His short-barreled .38 was on his left side, butt forward.

'Take it out and throw it on the floor,' Snyder said. 'Way over.'

Jesse tossed the .38 on the floor near the bread rack. Then he waited.

Snyder took a pull on the Chivas Regal.

'My life ain't worth shit to me,' Snyder said.

Jesse nodded.

'I got nothing to lose,' he said.

Jesse waited. Snyder was being dramatic, but self-dramatization was what this kind of situation was often about.

'So don't fuck with me,' Snyder said.

'That what you wanted to tell me?' Jesse said.

'I wanted to tell you that you fucked my life. I wanted to tell you I was married and we was happy until you.'

'Un-huh.'

'I wanted to fucking tell you that I'm going to kill her and then you and then maybe everybody else in this fucking store,' Snyder said.

'Un-huh.'

Snyder began to cry.

'I fucking loved her all my fucking life. Now she goes, I got fucking nothing.'

Mrs. Snyder's voice was barely a squeak.

'I won't go,' she said.

'Shut up. You already went, bitch.'

'You need help with this,' Jesse said. 'We can get you some help.'

'Help,' Snyder said. 'Fucking help. I'm her and she's me and you broke us up, you lousy fuck. You think you can get me help when my fucking life is completely fucking fucked?'

'It's not fucked yet,' Jesse said. 'Don't do something that will permanently fuck it.'

'I got no life without her,' Snyder said. 'She ain't leaving me. And I ain't leaving her. Ya unnerstan? Not fucking ever.'

He drank too big a drink from the bottle, and spilled some on his shirtfront. He was crying.

'We can help you with the booze,' Jesse said. 'We can still fix this.'

'Fix fuck,' Snyder said. 'All I got now is booze.'

He took another drink. Then he dropped the bottle and put his left arm around his wife's neck. He waved the handgun at Jesse.

'I'm going to shoot her,' he said.

Snyder started to thumb back the hammer. Only his face showed over his wife's shoulder. Jesse took the long-barreled .22 from the small of his back, leaned toward Snyder as he pulled it, and with his gun arm fully extended and steady, shot Snyder once through the middle of the forehead. It made a small, neat, dark hole. Mrs. Snyder stood still and screamed, as Snyder's arm went limp and slid off her neck and he fell over and lay still.

59

Jesse sat on his deck alone in the early evening. Still light. On the table next to him was a fifth of Dewar's and a bucket of ice and a big bottle of club soda. He held an unused glass in his hand, turning it slowly as he sat. The salt wind came tentatively off the harbor. There were cocktails being drunk on a couple of the cabin cruisers moored near the town dock. Jesse could hear a radio somewhere. A ball game. Probably the Sox. Funny how you could tell what it was by the sound of it, without quite being able to hear what was said. Across the harbor the pennants strung along the yacht club dock moved with the declining evening air.

Thank God it's ... what is today ... Tuesday. Thank God it's Tuesday.

He turned the glass in his hands. It was a squat glass, thick, with a hint of green.

He'd had to shoot him. Snyder would have done it.

He stood and put some ice in the glass. The ice took on the green tint even more faintly than the glass.

If he loved her so goddamned much, why was he going to shoot her?

He poured four ounces of scotch over the ice. The ice showed translucent through the amber scotch.

Maybe it wasn't love, maybe it was need.

He unscrewed the top of the soda bottle.

Which was not the same thing.

Jesse poured soda over the ice on top of the scotch.

So, if he needed her, why would he shoot her?

Jesse stirred his drink slowly by moving the ice cubes around with his forefinger. A rowboat moved across the surface among the moored boats. A man sat in the back. A boy was rowing. The boy was having trouble keeping the boat on course, but the man didn't seem bothered by it. He let the boy make his own adjustments. Jesse held his glass up and looked at the way the light came through it. There was moisture on the outside of the glass.

It was about control.

He could hear the water move below the deck. Occasionally he heard a seagull squawk. There was the faint sound of music to go with the ball game. And occasionally laughter from the partying power boats.

That was why Snyder beat her up. He had to know he could control her and then he could know he wouldn't lose her. Shooting her would be complete control.

Jesse swirled the glass a little, listening to the sound the ice cubes made against the glass.

The dumb bastard thought he loved her.

The rowboat reached the wharf and after a struggle the boy

166

brought it around so that it was against the landing float. The man reached out and held it steady while the boy climbed out. Then the boy held it steady for the man. Jesse made a gesture of toast toward them with his glass.

The man and boy took some tackle out of the rowboat and walked up the wharf and out of sight. Jesse sat turning his glass in his hands. Then he stood and walked to the railing of his deck and looked down at the cola-colored water rocking against the seawall below him and dropped his drink, glass and all, into the ocean.

60

Alan Garner was eating a slice of pepperoni pizza and drinking a diet Sprite at the counter of a place on Dartmouth Street when Jesse and Brian Kelly came in and sat down on either side of him.

Jesse said, 'Hi.'

Kelly didn't speak.

Garner looked for a moment at Jesse. Then he remembered.

'The police chief,' he said.

'Paradise, Mass.,' Jesse said.

Garner nodded.

'This is Detective Kelly,' Jesse said. 'Boston.'

'How ya doing,' Kelly said.

Garner chewed the last bite of his pizza, and wiped his mouth with a paper napkin. He swallowed some diet Sprite. Then he smiled.

'Am I in trouble with the law?' he said.

'You want to talk about it here?' Jesse said.

'We could sit in a booth,' Garner said.

'Sure.'

The two cops moved to a booth opposite the counter. Garner paid his bill, then he took his diet Sprite bottle and sat beside Jesse. Kelly sat across from them.

'So, guys, what's up?' he said.

'Tell us about Billie Bishop,' Jesse said.

'Who?'

'Billie Bishop,' Jesse said.

'I'm sorry, I don't know anything about Billie Bishop,' Garner said.

He took a little diet Sprite from the bottle, his elbow resting on the table so that he had to dip his head to drink.

'Tell us about Dawn Davis,' Jesse said.

Garner put his diet Sprite down.

'Dawn Davis,' he said.

'Dawn Davis,' Jesse said.

'I don't think I know her,' Garner said.

'How do you know it's a her?'

'I, oh, Dawn/Don, I see, I guess I just assumed because you were asking about a girl before.'

'Billie Bishop?' Kelly said.

'Yes.'

'How did you know Billie Bishop was a girl?' Kelly said.

Garner opened his mouth and closed it. He looked at his bottle of diet Sprite. He looked across at the counter man. Both cops were silent. Garner drank some diet Sprite. He looked at his watch.

'I … I don't have anything to say.'

'Where do you live?' Kelly said.

'Cohassett.'

'Where in Cohassett?'

'Jerusalem Road.'

'Where Gino Fish lives,' Kelly said.

'I live with Gino.'

'You his new tootsie?' Kelly said.

'We have a relationship,' Garner said.

'I'm glad for you,' Kelly said.

'And you work for him?' Jesse said.

'Yes.'

The cops didn't say anything.

'Why?' Garner said.

'Why what?' Jesse said.

'Why are you asking about Gino?'

Jesse took a small notebook from his pocket and thumbed through the pages for a moment.

'You used to live in Brighton?' Jesse said.

'Yes.'

'Market Street?'

'Yes. But I moved last year.'

'In with Gino,' Jesse said.

'Yes. There something wrong with that?'

'You remember your phone number in Brighton?'

'Five six ... something.'

Jesse read it to him.

'Could be it,' Garner said. 'You know how many numbers you have these days.'

Jesse read another number. 'How about that one?' he said.

'You must have checked that. It's my number at work.'

'In Gino's office,' Jesse said.

'Yes.'

Again they were silent. The diet Sprite bottle was empty. Garner looked at the door.

The poor bastard, Jesse thought. *He came in here, feeling good, going to have a nice piece of pizza, and now he's fucked and he knows it.*

The silence got longer.

Finally Garner said, 'What do you want?'

'We want to know what happened to Billie Bishop,' Jesse said.

'I don't know anything about that.'

Jesse looked at Kelly. Kelly sighed.

'Here's what we got,' Kelly said. 'We got you for procuring. We got you for living off the earnings of a prostitute. We got you for contributing to the delinquency of a minor. Probably several minors.'

Garner shook his head slowly as Kelly spoke.

'I don't know what you're talking about,' he said.

'We got a statement from Dawn Davis. We got a statement from T. P. Pollinger. We have your ass,' Kelly said.

'I want a lawyer,' Garner said.

'Sure,' Kelly said. 'As soon as we arrest you.'

'Maybe we can work something out,' Jesse said.

'Work out my ass,' Kelly said.

'Maybe he can help us,' Jesse said.

'Fuck him,' Kelly said.

'I want to know who killed Billie Bishop,' Jesse said.

'I don't know,' Garner said. 'I honest to God don't know.'

'Maybe you killed her,' Kelly said.

'No.'

'Maybe we could hang it on you anyway,' Kelly said.

'No.'

'Maybe,' Jesse said, 'what we need to do is to discuss this with Gino.'

'Gino?' Garner said.

'Sure. Since you were using his phone number, I figure you were doing it for him.'

'Gino's got nothing to do with this.'

'Really? You mean he doesn't know you're running an escort service for pedophiles out of his office?' Jesse said.

'Gino has nothing to do with this,' Garner said.

He looked scared.

'So, if he doesn't know,' Jesse said, 'and we tell him, maybe he'll be grateful and help us with our case.'

'Tell Gino?'

'Sure,' Jesse said.

Garner looked around the room. It was 2:20 in the afternoon. The counter man was talking through the serving window to the pizza chef. No one else was in the restaurant.

'No,' Garner said.

'No what?'

'You can't tell Gino.'

'Why not?'

'He'll kill me.'

'What a shame,' Kelly said.

Garner looked around the room again, as if he were looking for a way out. The two cops sat quietly. Jesse could hear Garner's breathing.

'If I tell you what I know,' Garner said, 'can you give me a break?'

'Of course,' Jesse said.

'And Gino doesn't have to know.'

'Mum's the word,' Jesse said.

'It started as nothing,' Garner said. 'A girl tried to pick me up. She was a kid. And I knew a guy liked kids, so I started talking to her and one thing led to another and I figured maybe she could use a little management.'

Garner fiddled with his empty bottle.

'She a runaway?' Jesse said.

'Yes. Was staying at the shelter in JP with the nun. So I started setting her up with guys,' Garner said. 'And we'd split.'

'How much did she get?' Kelly said.

'I did all the work,' Garner said. 'Took all the risks. Paid the rent, bought the clothes and makeup. All she had to do was have sex for half an hour or so.'

'So what'd she get? Ten cents on the dollar?'

Garner shrugged.

'So that was working pretty good, and I thought, hey, why not expand?' Garner smiled. 'The American way, you know?'

'And ...' Jesse said.

'I specialized. Young girls seem to like me. I'm fairly attractive, you know. And I don't seem threatening. So I started to, um, cull them from the shelters, and clean them up and ... put them in touch with clients.'

'And Gino didn't know.'

'It was before I met Gino.'

'When you were still living in Brighton.'

'Yes.'

'And when you moved in with Gino, you didn't want to give up your career.'

'I think it's important,' Garner said, 'for a boy to have an independent income.'

'Billie Bishop work for you?' Jesse said.

Kelly had leaned back in the booth with his arms crossed, looking without expression at Garner. His gaze was steady.

'Yes. I met her at the shelter.'

'She know you were in another program?' Jesse said.

Garner smiled.

'I'm in both programs,' he said.

'Doubles the odds for a date,' Kelly said, his stare steady on Garner.

'So the girls, like Billie Bishop, thought maybe you were their boyfriend,' Jesse said.

Garner nodded.

'Tell me about Norman Shaw,' Jesse said.

Garner sat back in the booth as if he'd been shoved.

'Norman Shaw?'

Jesse had his forearms resting on the tabletop, leaning toward Garner as he talked.

'Who's Norman Shaw?'

Neither Kelly nor Jesse spoke. Both sat as they had been sitting and waited.

After a long silence, Garner said, 'You mean the writer?'

Jesse made a brief smile. Garner looked as if he might be ill.

'I guess he's a friend of Gino's,' Garner said.

'Un-huh.'

Jesse raised his forearms from the table and put his clasped hands against his chin. Kelly was stone still.

'Can you keep me out of this?' Garner said.

'Absolutely,' Jesse said.

'I don't have to testify? Nothing?'

' 'Course not,' Jesse said.

Garner looked at Kelly. Kelly winked at him.

'I fixed Billie up with Mr. Shaw,' Garner said.

'Gino know?'

'Yes. Favor to Mr. Shaw. I told him Billie was just a kid I knew.'

'So Gino didn't know she was a hooker.'

'I don't know what Gino knew.'

'He know you were her pimp?'

'No. Absolutely not. I didn't take a dime from Mr. Shaw.'

'When did you give her to Shaw?' Jesse said.

'First time? Beginning of the summer.'

'You have any idea how she came to get killed?' Jesse said.

'Ohmigod, no,' Garner said.

'You think Gino would know?'

'No. I don't know. Gino doesn't know. You can't ask him. You promised.'

Neither cop spoke. The sound of Garner's breathing was loud and ragged.

Then Kelly spoke.

'You'll have to come over to the station,' Kelly said. 'Make a statement.'

'You promised.'

Kelly smiled and nodded at Jesse.

'Just a formality,' Kelly said. 'We need to cover ourselves.'

'I wouldn't want Gino to know,' Garner said.

Kelly didn't say anything.

'Nobody's going to know, right?' Garner said.

'Certainly not,' Jesse said.

Garner looked uncertain. The two cops were quiet.

'Your word?' Garner said.

'Absolutely,' Jesse said.

61

'I heard about how you shot a man,' Jenn said. 'It was on the wire at the station.'

Jesse nodded.

'How does that feel?' Jenn said.

'Necessary,' Jesse said.

They were in Jenn's living room. Sitting together on her couch. Jenn was drinking white wine. Jesse had a Pepsi.

'Oh, Mr. Laconic. You must feel more than that.'

'I try not to,' Jesse said.

'You need to experience your feelings, Jesse.'

'But I don't need to talk about them.'

'Are you angry? You sound angry.'

Jesse was quiet for a short time.

'Yes,' he said. 'I guess I maybe am.'

'At me?'

'No.'

Jenn leaned back against the arm of the sofa. She sipped a small amount of her wine, looking at Jesse over the rim of the glass.

'What?' she said.

Jesse stood and walked to the window and looked out. Then he turned and leaned against the wall beside the window.

'Feelings,' Jesse said, 'can really fuck you.'

Jenn raised her eyebrows and didn't say anything.

'Guy I shot,' Jesse said. 'Guy named Snyder ...'

Jenn nodded. Jesse noticed as he always did, how big her eyes were.

'He couldn't face it without being married to the woman he used to punch around.'

'He beat her up?' Jenn said.

'Regularly.'

'And she stayed with him?'

'For years,' Jesse said. 'I had something to do with her finally leaving him.'

'Why didn't she leave him sooner?'

'She didn't have anything else.'

'There must be something better than getting beat up all the time,' Jenn said.

Jesse shrugged. 'Poor bastard,' he said.

174

'Her? I should think she'd be glad he was gone.'

'Him,' Jesse said.

'Because he's dead?'

Jesse drank some Pepsi.

'Because he was so scared he'd lose her,' Jesse said, 'that he lost her.'

'Beating her up might not be the best way to keep her,' Jenn said.

'He had to control her. Unless he could control her she might leave.'

Jenn got up and poured herself a half a glass more wine. Then she sat back down on the couch and tucked her feet under her.

'And when she did leave he tried to force it more,' Jenn said.

'Yep.'

'He tell you this?'

'No.'

'You're guessing, then?'

Jesse shook his head.

'I'm not guessing,' he said.

Jenn had put her wineglass down on the coffee table. She had never cared if she drank or not, Jesse thought. *I wonder what that's like.*

'You're talking about you and me,' Jenn said.

'Maybe a little.'

'You've never hit me.'

'No. I never would,' Jesse said.

'But you know how he felt,' Jenn said.

'Something about the way I've clamped on to you,' Jesse said, 'you can't stand.'

'I love you, though.'

'I know that.'

'You're my best friend in the world,' Jenn said.

'I know that, too.'

Jesse finished his Pepsi and got another can. He brought the

175

can back from the kitchen and sat back down beside Jenn on the couch.

'Maybe if I could let you go,' Jesse said, 'then, maybe you could stay.'

'There are problems I need to solve, too,' Jenn said.

'Sure,' Jesse said. 'But I don't have to be one of them.'

Jenn put her hand out and pressed it against his cheek.

'The only way to have what you want is not to want it?' she said.

'Something like that.'

'And this man you shot,' Jenn said.

'Snyder.'

'He never learned that.'

'Nope.'

'And it killed him,' Jenn said.

'With a little help from me.'

62

Suitcase Simpson called Jesse at home at 10:15 in the evening.

'I'm at the motel,' Simpson said. 'Shaw's here.'

'Is he in a room?'

'One-twelve,' Simpson said. 'Just arrived. Knocked on the door and went in.'

'I'll be up.'

'Shall I stop him if he tries to leave?' Simpson said.

'No. I want to catch him in the act.'

It was 10:40 when Jesse pulled into the parking lot of the Boundary Suites motel. He drove through the big half-empty parking lot and parked a little ways from room 112. Simpson's Jeep was two cars away. Jesse walked to it.

'He still in there?' Jesse said.

'Yes.'

'Stay put,' Jesse said.

He walked to the motel lobby and flashed his badge at the night clerk.

'Room one-twelve,' he said. 'Who's registered?'

The clerk was slim with a thin mustache and a lot of dark hair. He wore yellow-tinted aviator glasses.

'Why do you want to know?' he said.

' 'Cause I'm the police,' Jesse said. 'Gimme a name.'

The clerk tapped for a moment on his computer and then read from the screen.

'Marsha Gottlieb,' he said.

'We need to open the room.'

The desk clerk didn't like it. But he didn't know what else to do. So he got a key and walked down to room 112 with Jesse. As they walked, Jesse gestured to Simpson, who joined them at the door.

'Don't knock,' Jesse said. 'Just unlock the door.'

'We always knock first,' the clerk said.

'Unlock it,' Jesse said.

The clerk shrugged as if to exonerate himself, put the master key in, and unlocked the door. Jesse pushed. It opened a few inches.

'Chain lock,' Jesse said. 'Do your stuff, Suit.'

Simpson put his shoulder down and lunged into the door. The screws holding the chain bolt pulled loose from the frame and the door slammed open. The lights were on. Shaw was on the bed with a young girl. Both were naked. Shaw just managed to roll off her as Jesse and Simpson came into the room. Jesse was holding his badge up. The desk clerk peered in after them.

'Beat it,' Jesse said to the clerk, and shut the door.

Simpson leaned against it.

Shaw was sitting up with a pillow over his lap to cover himself. The girl seemed frozen. There was a quart of vodka, a can of cranberry juice, some ice and two half-empty glasses on the bedside table.

'What do you want?' Shaw said.

Jesse could hear the panic in his voice. The girl lay still on the bed. Her eyes big. Her breasts had barely begun to show.

'How old are you?' Jesse said to the girl.

The girl shook her head and didn't say anything.

'I know you,' Shaw said.

'You should get under the covers,' Jesse said to the girl.

She kept staring at him, without any response.

'Get off the bed,' Jesse said to Shaw.

Shaw got up quickly and stood naked, with his pale belly sagging.

'What are you going to do?' he said.

Jesse pulled the spread loose on Shaw's side and folded it over the girl. He looked at Shaw.

'You don't have the right to just break in here like this,' Shaw said.

There was no force in his voice. He sounded plaintive.

'How old would you say she was?' Jesse said.

'Twenty-one,' Shaw said.

'She's jailbait,' Jesse said.

'She is not,' Shaw said. 'She told me she was twenty-one.'

'Put on your pants,' Jesse said.

He looked at the girl, still motionless under the spread. He looked around the room. There was some black underwear and a short floral sundress on one of the chairs. Jesse picked the clothes up and put them on the bed beside the girl.

'You need to get dressed, too,' he said.

The girl didn't move.

'You're not in trouble,' Jesse said to her. 'But we need you to go with us.'

Still she didn't move.

'If you don't get dressed,' Jesse said, 'we'll have to dress you.'

Wordlessly, she put the covers aside and got up and began to dress. Simpson looked carefully away.

'Where are we going?' Shaw said.

He was speaking slowly and very clearly, like a drunk pretending to be sober.

'We are going to jail,' Jesse said.

63

Joni Shaw came to her front door in a pale blue sundress.

'Well, hello,' she said.

'May I come in?' Jesse said.

'Of course.'

Carrying a manila envelope, Jesse walked through the gleaming air-conditioned house and sat again in the atrium.

'Thank you for calling last night,' she said.

Jesse nodded.

'Is Norman still in jail?'

'He'll be out this morning,' Jesse said. 'I wanted to talk with you first.'

'I'm not clear what he was arrested for. Drunk driving?'

'We found him in a motel room with an underage prostitute,' Jesse said.

He could hear Joni Shaw breathe in sharply.

'Oh, God!' she said.

'It's not the first time,' Jesse said.

She didn't say anything for a time. She studied Jesse's face as if she were looking for something.

'Are you sure?' she said finally.

Jesse opened the manila envelope and slowly spread out Dick Pettler's pictures of Shaw. Joni Shaw looked at them for a moment then pushed them away.

'Those are little girls,' she said.

'Yes.'

'How long ago were those pictures taken?'

'During a previous marriage,' Jesse said.

'I don't …' she said. 'I don't know what to say.'

'It gets worse,' Jesse said.

'Worse?' Joni Shaw said.

There was no way to ease it in.

'We're pretty sure he killed one of them.'

'Killed?'

'Does he own a gun?'

'A gun? You mean he shot someone?'

Jesse nodded. Joni Shaw had her arms folded across her chest as if she were hugging herself.

'Mother of God,' she said.

Jesse didn't want to bombard her. He waited for her to reorganize.

'You know this stuff?' she said.

'Yes.'

'Jesus,' she said. 'The fucking pervert.'

'Does he own a gun?' Jesse said.

'I guess I sort of knew it,' Joni Shaw said. 'You know how you know something and you don't know it?'

Jesse nodded.

'He was out a lot, and drunk nearly all the time,' she said.

Jesse nodded again.

'Look at me,' she said. 'If you were married to somebody like me, wouldn't you stay home nights?'

'Yes.'

'He wasn't a big deal in bed,' she said. 'All that stuff in the books? Bullshit! Most of the time he was too drunk to get it up.'

'Did he own a gun?' Jesse said gently.

'Probably too old for him,' she said. 'How old was the kid you caught him with last night?'

'She admits to fourteen.'

'Fourteen? Jesus Christ!' she said. 'Sick bastard.'

I'll circle the gun, Jesse thought.

'You love him?' he said.

Joni Shaw looked puzzled for a moment. She hunched her shoulders, still hugging herself.

'He's famous…. He's got money…. We didn't have much of

a sex life but he was nice to me most of the time....' She looked suddenly straight into Jesse's eyes. 'And sex is easy to get.'

'I would think so,' Jesse said.

'He was never ...' She paused. 'Thank you.'

'You're welcome,' Jesse said. 'He was never ... ?'

'He was never a mean drunk,' she said. 'And when he was sober he was really quite charming.'

'So it was a happy marriage.'

'Sure. He was a good provider. And I,' she said, 'made him look, ah, potent.'

'Did he own a gun?' Jesse said.

Joni looked at Jesse as if she'd never heard the question before.

'A gun?'

'Un-huh.'

'Yes,' she said. 'I'll show you.'

64

Kelly brought Alan Garner into Jesse's office at quarter to ten in the morning.

'Picked him up as soon as he came to open the office,' Kelly said.

'Gino know?'

'Not yet.'

Kelly leaned against the wall by the door and folded his arms. Garner stared at Norman Shaw. Shaw was sitting beside Jesse's desk. He had a bad hangover. His face was stiff. His movements were careful. His hands shook a little.

'I want a lawyer,' Garner said.

'You're not under arrest,' Jesse said.

'Then I want to leave.'

'Be in your best interest,' Jesse said, 'to stay.'

Garner looked at Kelly. Kelly shrugged.

'Long walk back to Boston,' he said.

'I want to call Gino.'

'Alan,' Kelly said. 'Right now we have you for a few small pimp charges. You might get away with no time.'

'We could jack that up to murder,' Jesse said.

Garner sat down, suddenly, beside Shaw. His face had gotten smaller. He had trouble swallowing.

'What murder?'

Shaw said, 'Should I have a lawyer?'

'I don't know,' Jesse said. 'Should you?'

'I haven't done anything,' Shaw said.

Jesse nodded.

'You know a kid named Billie Bishop?' Jesse said to Shaw.

'Of course not.'

'Why "of course not"?'

'Well, I mean, I know who I know, for God's sake.'

'And you don't know Billie Bishop?'

'No.'

Jesse looked at Garner.

'Alan?'

'What?'

'Does he know Billie Bishop?'

'You said I wouldn't …' Garner said. 'You promised I wouldn't have to testify.'

'I lied,' Jesse said. 'Does he know Billie Bishop?'

'I can't … Gino …'

'One of you will go down for this,' Jesse said. 'You want to be it?'

'Down for what?'

'Killing the kid,' Jesse said.

'I didn't kill anybody.'

Jesse waited. Kelly was still and expressionless leaning on the door. Shaw seemed to have shrunk in his chair.

'I just introduced him to her.'

'Shaw to Billie?' Jesse said.

Shaw made a stifled sound as if he'd been hit.

'Yes.'

'You deliver?'

'Deliver?'

'Do you bring the girls to Shaw?'

'Usually yes. I mean, these girls don't usually have a car.'

'And if they did they're not old enough to drive,' Kelly said.

'Every one of them told me she was at least twenty,' Shaw said suddenly.

His voice seemed high and unnatural, almost petulant. Nobody responded.

'And you drive them to the motel?'

'Yes. And give them money to register. No credit card, you know? Cash in advance.'

'This isn't what it sounds like,' Shaw said. 'I'm thinking of doing a book on prostitution.'

'You own a gun?' Jesse said.

'A gun?' Shaw's voice was almost a squeak.

'A gun.'

'No, I don't.'

Jesse opened the drawer of his desk and took out the gun Shaw's wife had given him and put it on the desk so Shaw could see it. Shaw looked at it without speaking. Jesse waited. Leaning against the wall, Kelly smiled like a happy wolf. He waited. Alan Garner sat absolutely still, trying to attract no attention.

'That's not my gun,' Shaw said finally, his high voice shaking.

'How could it be?' Jesse said. 'If you don't own one.'

'That's right,' Shaw said.

Jesse was quiet again, looking at Shaw. Shaw tried to hold his gaze and couldn't and looked around the office in a dreadful parody of unconcern.

'Do you have any coffee?' Shaw said.

Jesse said, 'No.'

Everyone was silent again. Shaw couldn't keep from looking

at the gun on Jesse's desk. After a time Jesse spoke. His voice sounded too loud to him.

'I found the gun in your desk,' Jesse said.

'You were looking in my desk?'

'Your wife and I,' Jesse said.

'She showed you?'

'Yes.'

'She knows?'

'Yes.'

'About the girls?'

'Yes.'

Shaw looked as if he wanted to say something, but nothing was there to be said.

'You dumb fuck,' Jesse said. 'You didn't clean it. There was a round missing. You didn't even reload.'

Again Shaw started to speak and failed. Finally he said, 'I need a drink.'

There was a tape recorder on Jesse's desk. Jesse turned it on.

'Why'd you kill her, Norman?'

Shaw sat back in his chair, his shoulders slumped, his hands clasped between his thighs.

'She said she was going to tell on me,' he said.

His voice wasn't high anymore, but it remained petulant.

'A high school dropout,' he said. 'She said she didn't like some of the things we did.'

'You were paying for those things,' Jesse said encouragingly.

'That's right, and this little dropout whore … I'm a best-selling author. I had too much to lose.'

Shaw stopped.

'You shoot her?' Jesse said.

Shaw didn't answer. 'God,' he said. 'I need a drink.'

'You shoot her?'

Shaw's voice sounded hoarse. 'Yes,' he said.

65

They were in Swampscott, walking on Fisherman's Beach, near where they had first eaten lunch together. Jesse was chewing gum.

'How did Billie's parents react?' Lilly said.

'The old man got up without saying anything and walked out of the house. The mother didn't flinch. Told me she'd lost her daughter a long time ago.'

'God,' Lilly said. 'What about the other one? The one who brought him the girls?'

'Alan Garner.'

'Yes.'

'Gino Fish will find out he's been running a child prostitution ring out of Gino's office,' Jesse said. 'He won't be around long enough to prosecute.'

'His boss will fire him?'

'His boss will kill him.'

'Kill him?'

Jesse nodded.

'You know that and you'll let it happen?' Lilly said.

'I can't prove he's going to do it.'

'But you know it,' Lilly said.

'Sure.'

'But …' Lilly paused and her eyes widened. 'You want it to happen. Don't you?'

'Garner isn't much of a guy,' Jesse said.

They were quiet. The tide was out. The beach was wide and firm and easy to walk on. A couple of terns moved ahead of them, cocking heads occasionally, then hopping on.

'That's the part of you that doesn't show much,' Lilly said.

Jesse smiled. 'I beg your pardon,' he said.

'Not that part. It's the cold part of you – without sentiment, without mercy. It is frightening.'

'People are more than one thing,' Jesse said.

'I know,' Lilly said. 'I didn't mean that as critically as it sounded. I know you can feel compassion. I know you found that girl's killer, partly because you felt somehow you owed it to her.'

'I'm also employed to do that,' Jesse said.

'And maybe the scary part of you – the remorseless part, the part that looks at the world with an icy stare – maybe that part of you is why you can do what you're employed to do.'

'Maybe,' Jesse said.

They were walking the beach at the margin where the sand was hardest. The ocean eased up toward them as they walked and almost reached them and lingered and shrank back, and eased up toward them again. Lilly stopped and stared out at the ocean. Jesse stood beside her.

'Long way out,' Jesse said.

They stood silently together looking at the horizon.

'Where are we going, you and I?' Lilly said.

'Back to your place?' Jesse said. 'Where I show another hard side of myself.'

Lilly smiled. 'Probably,' she said.

The easy wind off the ocean blew her silvery hair back from her young face and pressed her white cotton dress tight against her chest and thighs.

'But I meant *where are we going?* more like, ah, metaphorically.'

'You mean what about our future?'

'Yes.'

'Like walk into the sunset?'

'Yes.'

Jesse put his head back so that he was squinting up at the sky. He chewed his gum slowly. The tide was coming in. The reach of the ocean water had forced them back a step.

'I think I love you, Jesse.'

Jesse's jaw moved gently as he chewed the gum. The two terns that had been shadowing them flew up suddenly and slanted out over the ocean.

'If I can be with Jenn,' Jesse said after a time, 'I will be.'

Out from shore, a lobster boat chugged past them heading toward Phillips Beach.

'Even if you are together again,' Lilly said at last, 'maybe we could still have our little ... arrangement.'

Jesse took a deep breath. He liked Lilly a lot. In bed she was brilliant. With her he felt less alone than he had since Jenn left. He let the breath out slowly.

'Maybe not,' he said.

66

Jesse still used a wooden bat. The ball jumped off the aluminum ones much farther, but they didn't give the feeling of entirety, in the hands and forearms, that a wooden bat did. Jesse was playing tonight in shorts and a sleeveless tee shirt. His gun and badge were locked, with his wallet, in the glove compartment of his car. There was a league rule against wearing spikes, so they played in colorfully ornamented sneakers. And Jesse didn't wear batting gloves. He had worn them when he played in the minors, because everyone did, and it hadn't occurred to him not to. But in a twilight softball league they seemed pretentious to him.

Jesse planted his feet in the holes that had already been worn there. But Jesse wasn't uncomfortable. He had never been uncomfortable playing ball. Playing ball was like being home.

He took a pitch wide for a ball.

When you were going good, he remembered, the ball had come up there slowly, looking the size of a cantaloupe. He smiled to himself. Now it was about the size of a cantaloupe. He took a shoulder-high pitch for a strike. He glanced back once at the umpire. The umpire shrugged. Jesse grinned. He'd get a make good in one of these at bats.

He's pitching high and low, Jesse thought. *Next time he'll be down.*

The wind off the lake swirled a little dust between home and the pitcher's mound. Jesse stepped out. The infield was well over to the left side. The outfield was around to the left and deep. In this league he was a power hitter. Jesse got back in the box.

The next pitch came in thigh high, where Jesse was looking for it, and when he swung he could feel the exact completeness of the contact up into his chest. He dropped the bat and, without looking, began to trot slowly toward first.

Suitcase Simpson, coaching at first, said to him, 'Three trees back toward the restaurant.'

The opposing third baseman said, 'Nice home-run trot.'

There were a half dozen people in the stands behind third base. As he came into third, Jesse looked at them. One of them was Joni Shaw. She waved at him. He grinned at her, and ran on home.

MICHAEL BRANDMAN & THE SAGA OF JESSE STONE

In late 1996, after repeated prodding, Robert B. Parker's long time film agent, Flora Roberts, finally arranged for me to meet Bob for breakfast at his favorite Los Angeles hotel. We started talking at around nine am and, by noon, we were still at it. That's when Joan Parker joined us. Then the three of us talked our way through lunch and well into the afternoon. It was the beginning of a dialogue which would continue for the rest of Bob's life. There was no subject we didn't exhaust. There was no such thing as a short conversation. We were never at a loss for raucous laughter.

Bob's erudition was legion; his knowledge prodigious; his passions profound. He had the answer for every question. And more importantly, that answer came accompanied by his skewed and ironic perspective. Bob had a passion for movies. Old ones. He had long since given up venturing out to see any of the new ones. Even those which came highly recommended. Regardless, it wasn't long before we began making movies together. We even wrote together, most notably the re-make of Jack Schaefer's *Monte Walsh*, which now starred a popular actor by the name of Tom Selleck.

Prior to its publication, Bob showed me the manuscript of his novel *Stone Cold*, and we both agreed it would be the perfect movie fit for Selleck. Inasmuch as Tom Selleck, Bob and I had already worked together, both on Louis L'Amour's *Crossfire Trail*, and on *Monte Walsh*, the three of us met to discuss it. Tom immediately climbed aboard. In short order, we sold the project to CBS, thus beginning the franchise of Jesse Stone movies which still continues to thrive.

Jesse Stone became the most significant character Tom had played since Magnum. *Stone Cold* was a huge success. CBS quickly ordered more. And with each successive movie, Tom and I became more involved in the writing. Our editorial guru was Bob, whose comments and ideas always made us better. In addition to *Stone Cold*, I co-wrote the screenplays for *No Remorse*, *Death in Paradise*, *Innocents Lost* and the forthcoming *Benefit of the Doubt*. I co-wrote the story for *Thin Ice*, and supervised the writing for both *Sea Change*, and *Night Passage*. Along with Tom Selleck, I co-executive produced them all. It was due to my having written in part on these Jesse Stone movies that Putnam proposed I succeed Bob in the writing of the novels, a thought which would never have occurred to me. Following in the footsteps of a Grand Master is daunting enough, but when that Grand Master is Robert B. Parker, it's positively dizzying. But I came to realize that my experiences with Bob had helped shape me as a writer. We had discussed in great detail what it was like for him to write Raymond Chandler. The sparseness of Chandler's language, his humor, the richness of his characters, his heightened sense of irony... all had informed and influenced Bob.

Having read everything Bob had written helped to inform and to guide me as I was writing *KILLING THE BLUES*. I can't even begin to describe how humbling and profound an experience it was. Joan Parker recently commented that from whatever cloud Bob's now sitting on, he is most assuredly amused that it's I who is carrying his torch. I'm only hoping that he's not press-checking his pistol and preparing to fire at me.

Truth is, I'd much rather be with Bob in Lucy's El Adobe, the Mexican cantina in Los Angeles...sitting beneath the photos of him which hang on the wall, pigging out on enchiladas and margaritas...which we did shamelessly in the middle of the day...laughing and carrying on as was our wont.

So, I am honored to have been chosen as the guardian of the Jesse Stone escutcheon. And terrified as well. Robert B. Parker was an American original. There was no one else like Bob. He was smart, funny, tart, ironic, generous, garrulous and singular. He brooked no fools and made no amends. He was a writer, singer, actor, boxer, tough guy, family man, pussy cat.

I am so very proud to have been Bob Parker's friend, and now to have been chosen to carry on the Jesse Stone legacy.

Robert B. Parker's résumé is familiar to most of his readers. Born and raised in Massachusetts, graduated from Colby College in Maine, married Joan Hall, had two sons, earned his Ph.D. at Boston University, taught at Northeastern University, and wrote nearly seventy books.

There are other factoids about him that are less well known. Bob's talent for rhythm was first put to work when the U.S. Army sent him to Korea as a Morse code radio operator. He always wanted to be a writer, but he needed a steady income to support his young wife and, later, his sons. Bob was hired as a technical writer first for Raytheon and then for Curtiss-Wright, which soon laid him off. He next worked as editor of a magazine for Prudential insurance agents and freelanced as a partner in Parker/Farman, the "world's smallest advertising agency."

Unable to take any more of corporate America, and with no interest in advertising, Bob returned to school. The plan was to earn a doctorate, get a job teaching, and have the time to start writing seriously. While going to school, he held down as many as five college teaching jobs at once, often took care of his sons, and did odd jobs for a consulting company. Fortunately for the family, Joan had a job in education that paid well.

The plan worked, and as a teacher at Northeastern University, Bob found the time to write. He was one of four authors of an anthology textbook, *The Personal Response to Literature*, published in 1971. Two years later, the first Spenser novel, *The Godwulf Manuscript*, appeared.

Bob was renowned for his Spenser novels, featuring the wise-cracking, street-smart Boston private-eye, which earned him a devoted following and reams of critical acclaim. He also launched two other bestselling series featuring, respectively, Massachusetts police chief Jesse Stone and Boston private detective Sunny Randall. In addition, he authored four Westerns.

Bob's bestselling Western novel *Appaloosa* was made into a major motion picture by New Line, starred Ed Harris and Viggo Mortensen, and was a box office hit in 2008. Long acknowledged as the dean of American crime fiction, he was named Grand Master of the Edgar Awards in 2002 by the Mystery Writers of America, an honor shared with earlier masters such as Alfred Hitchcock and Ellery Queen.

Robert B Parker died in 2010 at the age of 77.